MACHINES OF THE DEAD 2

DAVID BERNSTEIN

CHAPTER 1

"Dammit." Jack slammed his fist against the outboard motor.

Twenty minutes after escaping New York City and almost becoming zombie chow, the speedboat's engine stopped working. Jack looked at Zaun, who was finally waking up. Maria had conked him on the head pretty hard.

"What happened?" he groaned.

Jack came over and knelt next to him. "Maria knocked you out. How are you feeling?"

"Bitch." Zaun put a hand to the back of his neck. "Ouch."

Jack stood. "You'll be fine. Maria didn't want you causing trouble and wasting anymore time." Looking back at the engine, he shook his head. "I think we're screwed."

Zaun grunted as he got to his feet. "Where are we and why aren't we moving?"

"Engine gave out, and won't start back up."

"Fuel?"

"Plenty. I guess, out of the three available boats, we picked a dud."

A strong, cold gust blew across the craft, causing it to rock wildly.

"Damn, it's cold out here," Zaun said.

Jack eyed the river ahead, then pointed. "That's the Tappan Zee Bridge. We're only about forty minutes from Cornwall, from Sara."

"Yeah," Zaun said. "Forty minutes by boat, but if we have to go by foot, it'll take much longer and be a hell of a lot more dangerous."

"You're not wrong about that," Jack agreed.

"And getting to shore might take a while. The current isn't looking so strong. For now, we're stuck in the middle of the Hudson."

"Could be worse," Jack said, hearing the negativity in Zaun's voice. "We could still be in the city, or worse, members of those bot-controlled corpses. Fucking Reynolds."

Memories of their horrible time in the city flooded his mind. He couldn't believe it had all started only a month ago with his wife getting infected and dying, then coming back to life. She had been a victim of Dr. Reynolds' escaped patient. The crazy escapee ran through the city, biting and infecting people. The contagion, tiny microscopic machines, spread like wildfire, animating people's corpses when they died.

Seemed like only yesterday when Jack and his wife, Jess, were walking down the sidewalk together, getting ready to head home for a relaxing weekend. And all the time they lived in the apartment, Dr. Reynolds and his secret lab had been right under their building, performing human experiments for the military. It was only for that reason Jack survived. If he'd been in another building, he would have been left topside by Reynolds' team, to try and survive, or die like most of Manhattan's residents.

The whole "bot" program seemed like a good idea. Create microscopic robots to aid soldiers in battle and to help in the healing and regrowth of limbs. But it had first been designed as a weapon—a "bug" that could be sent into an area and spread quickly. The dead would reanimate and infect others, creating extreme chaos and confusion. The infected area would be quarantined. It was the perfect weapon.

When Dr. Reynolds was finally able to use it to try and help soldiers heal, he went about it all wrong. He used human test subjects, taking the homeless off the streets and promising them money for their time.

After the contagion hit Manhattan and grew out of control, Reynolds' "test subjects" dried up. Jack, Zaun and a new friend, Maria Lopez—one of the guards at the bunker, were to become the next subjects of Reynolds' experiment. From there, Jack and the others had one goal: to escape the city. Maria had a daughter to get home to in North Carolina. Jack had a sister in Cornwall, New

York, whom he hadn't spoken to in over a year. The small group made it out of Manhattan and to a fenced-in area topside where Reynolds' operation kept speedboats. Jack and Zaun went one way, while Maria went south to get to her little girl.

Jack couldn't believe what they'd all been through. They had become like a family, and now Maria was gone, and he and Zaun were stranded.

"So," Zaun said, "are we going to try and swim for the shore?"

With the wind gusting and the temperature around 20 degrees Fahrenheit, feeling more like 10 degrees with the wind, jumping into the water was not going to be an option. And it wasn't actually being in the water that would be the worst part. It would be when they reached the shore. They'd be frozen in minutes, eternal sleep moments away. There would be no dry clothes to change into. They would have to light a fire quickly before they froze, and there just wasn't going to be time, at least Jack didn't imagine so.

"I think it's best to wait here for now," he said. "We're safe and dry. Hopefully we'll drift to shore, if not at least get closer to it."

Jack and Zaun huddled in the boat's cramped cabin, leaving the door open to listen for sounds—another boat's engine or maybe even an airplane. Without the wind blowing on them, both men warmed a bit.

The truth was that Jack had no idea how far the bot-virus had spread. Maybe it was contained to the Northeast. With no way of knowing, and needing to get to his sister, he had to survive and push on. When nightfall arrived, the temperature was going to drop. He could only hope to reach land by then. He and Zaun could use the boat as shelter and start a fire.

"You shouldn't have let her go," Zaun finally said after a bout of silence.

"You'd have stopped her?" Jack said, blowing into his hands.

Zaun opened his mouth to speak, but nothing came out. Then, "No, but we could've figured something out."

Jack shook his head. "She has a daughter to get to. I have a sister. It sucks, but we have different priorities."

"We should have stayed together. Figured something out. We've got no idea what the rest of the area is like, hell, the country. We were stronger having her with us."

"I agree. Having us all together would've been great. But would it have been right to ask her to delay finding her daughter? Or for me to forget about my sister and go hundreds of miles in another direction? You're a free agent. You can go anywhere, but she thought it was best that you and I stay together."

Zaun sighed. "Well, whatever. It's done now. She's gone."

Jack nodded.

They sat in silence for a while, the boat rocking gently as it slowly drifted.

Jack missed Maria already. Knowing he'd probably never see her again was disheartening. She was a great person and a warrior. They'd all been through so much together. They would be bonded for life. He hated seeing her go, but she had loved ones to find.

He thought about their escape.

In the beginning, the entire island of Manhattan was quarantined. The airways were controlled by aircraft, Black Hawk helicopters, and fighter jets. The waterways were patrolled by military attack boats, armed with machine guns and rocket launchers. Bridges and tunnels were sealed off. So how had the contagion spread? The answer was simple. People must have escaped. Jack and the others had a secret underground tunnel to use, making their exodus easy. He wondered how others made it out. Maybe friends in the army or through tunnels, like old forgotten subway lines and sewers.

So many questions ran through his mind, but for now, the only thing he cared about was getting to his sister's house. Like himself, she was a survivor. Her husband, an abusive asshole had been the reason they hadn't spoken in over a year. She'd needed his help. He should've realized it, but instead he let her be. If...no, *when* he found her, he'd tell her how sorry he was she was trapped in that terrible relationship, and whatever she needed, he would be there for her.

He only prayed she was still alive.

CHAPTER 2

Maria fought back tears as she sped away from Jack and Zaun. She missed them already, and felt as if she were leaving a part of her family. They had been through so much together, and now it was time to go their separate ways. But crying? She wasn't a crier. Not really anyway. Maybe it was just the unknown she was heading into that was getting to her. She had no clue what to expect with each passing moment. The contagion had spread from Manhattan to the outer boroughs of Brooklyn and Queens, which were part of the island of Long Island. But had it spread across the bridges to Upstate New York? To the west, Pennsylvania? South to New Jersey? Maybe it never reached the mainland. Looking around, she didn't think she'd be that lucky. There were no planes in the air, or boats guarding the waters. Things must have completely collapsed.

The bot-virus had spread fast, killing a human and turning them into an undead corpse within a day. Reynolds had said they were designed to adapt. They could be stronger now and harder to kill.

Maria thought of her daughter and it made heading off alone that much more tolerable. She would face anything and anyone in order to get to her daughter. Maria had left her little girl in good hands with her brother and mother while she was serving her country. If the contagion had hit North Carolina, her brother, a former marine, would know what to do, know how to survive, and they would all be okay.

What she had gone through in New York City was an anomaly. The rest of the world, having seen what happened, would be more prepared. How could they not be? Her family would be fine.

Jack and Zaun would be too, and she planned on catching up with them again when everything was back to normal, or at least under control. A little voice kept pestering her, asking her *if things would get back to normal. Maybe the world was screwed and things would never be the same again. Maybe Jack and Zaun were as good as dead. Maybe her family . . .* No, she couldn't let those thoughts overwhelm her. She needed to remain positive, like when she was out on the battlefield and in hostile territory. Worrying was difficult not to do, but ultimately, it didn't help. She would have to rely on her military training, and keep her emotions from getting the best of her.

She anchored her fears and concentrated on driving the boat, keeping an eye out for whatever may come her way, and how great it would be to have her daughter in her arms.

A thud from below caught her attention. She paused, listening. Then the cabin doors flew open and a man, one of Reynolds' crew, came charging up the stairs. He was holding a handgun and pointed it at Maria's face. "Shut the boat down, now."

Maria froze, completely taken off guard. It didn't happen often, but this was a shocker.

The man was Mark Saunders, a guard from the bunker. She had talked to him a few times, coming away with the impression that the man was not just an asshole, but certifiable.

Saunders backhanded her, knocking her into the seat behind the wheel. He stepped up, keeping his Px4 Berretta pointed at her. He lowered the throttle, then killed the engine. "Hand me your sidearm, soldier. Slowly."

Maria glared at him. Her right cheek burned where he hit her. She had been careless in assuming the boat was unoccupied. With everything going on—the undead, being pursued by a madman's group of soldiers—she should've known better. The bastard must have seen them approaching the boathouse, knew he was out-gunned, and hid—not having enough time to start the engine and get away.

"I'm not going to ask again," Saunders said, shoving the .40 in her face.

Maria reached for her sidearm, a Glock 21. The man's arm tensed. He took a step back. She held the weapon out like someone might hold a dead rat. Saunders grabbed the gun and tucked it into his pants.

"We're not enemies. Reynolds is dead. New York has fallen. We should be helping each other get out of here."

Saunders laughed.

"What's so funny?" Maria asked.

"New York has fallen?" he asked. "Sweetie, the whole country has fallen, or will be soon enough. Along with Canada and Mexico."

"What are you talking about? No way this thing spread that fast. The military would never allow it to get that far."

"Stay there," he told her and walked toward the back of the boat. She turned and saw him head to the outboard motor. He bent, opened a panel on the side of it, then flipped a red switch. "That ought to do it."

"Do what? We should be getting the hell out of here."

He shut the panel and stood. "Believe me, I'd like nothing more than to get out of here, but what's the rush? A few minutes more and we'd have been blown out of the water. I feel reborn."

"Blown out of the water? Why?"

"Boat's rigged with explosives. Engine's got a failsafe built-in. Someone steals a boat, they go boom!"

Jack. Zaun.

Maria's insides grew cold. Her heart pounded a little harder. Her friends were in trouble. Maybe even dead.

"What's the matter?" Saunders asked, smiling. "You worried about your friends?"

Maria glared at him.

"Well, don't," he said. "I'm sure they're long dead by now, or at least on their way to being dead, burning to crispy critters."

"What do you want from me?"

"The world is going to hell. I figure I better keep you for myself. Can't be too many good-looking women around." He grinned.

"We'll find us a nice place and hole up. Live off the land. Have some kids, and stay the hell away from the undead. Now, get up."

The guy was nuts. Had flipped out. Reynolds' track record for hiring psychos was spot on. As much as she didn't want to admit it, Saunders was probably correct; most likely her friends were dead by now, but she still had to try and save them."

"I said to get up," he repeated himself, pointing his gun at her.

"Where are we going?"

He motioned to the cabin doors. "Down there. We're going to make love. Get started on making us a family. Have to start over now, you know?"

The guy was obviously out-of-it, but Maria thought that might be a good thing. He wasn't thinking clearly, hadn't patted her down. She still had her knife in her boot.

Saunders grabbed Maria by her hair and yanked her up. He held her close. She felt his warm breath cascade over her ear. He grinned wickedly, then shoved her down the steps. She stumbled and crashed into one of the open doors. Pain radiated in her right shoulder, but she managed to crawl into the cabin. With nowhere else to go, she rolled onto her back.

Saunders came down the stairs, his body all but a shadowy figure. "Time to get naked," he said.

She saw that he still held the Beretta. "You don't need the gun. I'll do whatever you want."

"That's because I *have* the gun." He laughed. "But in time, that will change. You'll learn to love me and our children." He kneeled down, untied his right boot, then his left, and kicked them off.

Maria inched backwards.

"Where are you going?" Saunders asked, as he removed his jacket. His shirt came off next, revealing a muscled hairy chest. Tattoos of a lion's head and an eagle in flight covered his pectorals.

Maria went to stand, but he cut her short. Shaking his head, he said, "No, no."

She looked at him. It was so cold and he didn't seem to care. Maybe he'd get frost bite and become ill. Problem was it wouldn't be fast enough. She was going to have to fight.

"On your knees," he said.

Maria did as she was told.

"Now, come to me."

She knee-crept along the floor until she reached him, her head at crotch level. Saunders placed the barrel of his gun against her temple. "Unzip me."

Maria's heart pounded. Anger coursed through her veins like nitrous oxide fueling her with the desire to maim. Her fingers curled into claws. The barrel pressed harder against her skull.

"Try anything stupid and I'll blow your brains out. Then I'll fuck your corpse. I'm getting some either way."

Maria shivered, unsure if it was from the cold or the image of the man violating her dead body. She couldn't do it. Couldn't lay with this man. Let him invade her.

But that wasn't true because she needed to survive, for herself and her daughter. Somehow, she knew her little girl was alive and she could and would do anything to get back to her.

Saunders grabbed onto her hair and shoved her face into his crotch. Maria struggled, inhaling the stench of old urine. She needed to gag. The man let go and she pulled back, gulping fresh air.

Anger continued to course through her body. She looked up at him, her eyes piercing.

"I see how angry you are, but that'll pass. You'll see that I'm a good lover and a good man. Just go with it for now." His expression turned serious. "Now, do your duty as my new wife, or after I'm done with you, I'll toss you overboard for the fish."

Maria reached up, pinched the zipper of his pants between her fingers and pulled down. The sound echoed in her ears for what seemed like an eternity. The acrid smell of urine wafted out, stronger than ever now. She cringed. There was no way she was putting his thing in her, let alone in her mouth.

Forcing a smile, she looked up at him.

"I haven't had a chance to wash in awhile, but it's all good," he said, grinning.

Maria smiled wider, keeping eye contact, and slid her left hand into his pants. She rubbed him through his underwear and felt him stiffening. His eyes softened and his lips parted. He let out a groan of pleasure. "That's nice. Real nice."

She needed him to close his eyes, if only for a second. Swallowing back the disgust, she slid her hand into his briefs and grabbed his clammy flesh. Though the barrel was still pressed against her head, the pressure had lessened. Saunders let out an "ahhhh" and closed his eyes.

Maria reached down with her right hand and slid the knife from her boot. Saunders opened his eyes and stared at her. "Keep going," he said, "but do it slow."

He undid the button on his pants. They slid down, leaving only his briefs as the remaining barrier. Her hand was still inside, holding him. She felt the bile rise in her throat and fought to keep from puking. It was now or never. In one movement, she swatted his gun hand out of the way and brought the knife up, sinking it into his groin. He screamed. The gun went off. She pulled out the blade, her body numb. She had no idea where the bullet went—into her? Into the floor? The wall? It didn't matter. She stabbed him again, and again and again, watching his underwear turn from white to red.

Saunders continued to wail. He was pushing against her, trying to get her off, but she was strong—unstoppable. The damage was done, but she kept plunging the blade in, blood gushing over her hand. Then he hit her. The side of her head exploded in pain as she was thrown sideways. She hit the side of a seat cushion, the thin foam doing little to soften the blow. The knife fell from her grip as she landed on the floor. Slightly dazed, she glanced up and saw her attacker, his crotch a bleeding mess. But better yet, he was no longer holding the gun. It was on the floor at his feet. She dove, snatched the weapon, rolled backwards, and came up into a crouching position with the gun held out.

Saunders was on his knees, holding his groin. Tears streamed down his face. He started laughing as he stared at her. "Fucking bitch," he said, spittle flying from his mouth. He put a foot forward, grunting as he stood. Maria's mouth dropped open. The guy was fierce. She didn't think he'd be able to stand, but he did. "I'm going to kill you."

Maria squeezed the trigger on the Beretta. A small hole appeared in the man's chest. He staggered back, then looked down at the wound. A trickle of blood leaked out. He looked at her as rage enveloped his face. He reached out, then fell forward, crashing to the floor. She wanted to shoot him again, but couldn't risk putting a hole in the boat's floor. She quickly felt for a pulse and didn't find one. The immediate danger was out of the way, but now she had another problem.

She headed out of the cabin and to the steering wheel. Her gun was resting on the chair. The cocky bastard had left it there. She stuffed it into her pants and started the boat, then raced in the opposite direction, hoping to reach Jack and Zaun in time.

CHAPTER 3

Zaun had fallen asleep. Jack was growing weary, trying not to nod off. The rhythmic rocking of the boat combined with the cold and silence was hard to fight. He took out the wedding picture of him and Jess. His heart swelled. Tears rimmed his eyelids and he blinked them away.

"I miss you so much," he whispered, then kissed the photo. No matter how hard he tried to survive, to live, he knew he'd never get a chance to hold her again. The thought was so outrageous, yet so true. He knew this, but couldn't fully accept it yet. Maybe he would see her again . . . in Heaven. He had never been a religious fellow, but Jess was his soul mate. Whether it was his brain telling him what he needed, or some kind of spiritual sensation, he truly felt that one day he'd get to be with her.

A low buzzing startled him but he remained still, holding his breath, and allowing his ears to focus completely. It was an engine, a boat's engine. He tucked the picture back into his jacket pocket and nudged Zaun.

"What's going on?" Zaun asked, sleepily.

"Grab your gun. We have company."

Jack grabbed his M4, the weapon was like an extension of him now, and something he didn't picture being without. He opened the cabin doors and crept up the stairs, peering just over the top step.

"Sounds like a boat," Zaun said.

"It is. Wait here. Might be better if they think I'm alone. We'll have the element of surprise."

The approaching craft was identical to the one he and Zaun were on. Then he saw the familiar face. He turned back to Zaun. "It's

Maria." He couldn't help but smile, overjoyed at seeing her, but at the same time he knew it couldn't be good news. Something bad must've happened.

"Maria? What?" Zaun asked.

Jack stood on the deck, keeping the machine gun ready in the event Maria was under duress. Zaun was at his side in moments.

Maria pulled the boat alongside Jack's. It rested lower in the water, which he found odd. "You have no idea how glad I am to see you two."

"What's wrong?" Jack asked, a creeping feeling in his gut.

"You both need to get off the boat now." Maria's face was all business. "The engine's rigged with explosives."

"What are you talking about?" Zaun asked.

"Explosives?" Jack asked.

"Just get over here," Maria said, her voice urgent, "I'll explain everything."

Jack and Zaun gathered their things and boarded Maria's craft. She hit the throttle and sped off, stopping a little over a hundred yards away, then killed the engine.

"Reynolds had all the boats rigged with explosives. There's a kill-switch on the engine."

Jack's eyes went wide. "That crazy son-of-a-bitch!"

"I thought you guys were dead. The explosives are set to go off when the boat reaches a certain distance."

"We were cruising along," Jack began, "and then the engine just died."

"I think you got lucky," Maria said. "Very lucky."

Both Jack and Zaun thanked her. Jack was a little shaken. Something electrical or mechanical must've gone wrong, preventing the bomb from detonating, from killing them. Or maybe the engine cutting out had stopped it. They were a good distance from the boathouse. Truth was he had no idea why the thing hadn't exploded, but he was grateful.

"So, how far is Cornwall from here?" Maria asked.

"I can't ask you to take us there," Jack said. "You've got a long trip south. It's enough you came back for us."

Maria grinned. "You'd rather swim or hike there? Maybe find a vehicle . . . that's of course after fighting off either the undead or other people you might run into. Then you'll have to make your way along the streets and you have no idea if they're clogged or not. "

As much as Jack hated to admit it, she was right. By boat, Cornwall was maybe forty-five minutes, or an hour at most. She could let them off there and then be on her way.

"You'll use a lot of gas getting us there," Jack said. "If we don't find a refueling dock, you'll have to wait until we find gas cans and fill them. And we don't even know if there will be electricity. The pumps won't run without it."

"I don't have enough to get to North Carolina anyway. I'll need to stop a few times. An hour added onto my trip isn't all that terrible, and I'll rest easier knowing you're where you need to be."

Jack shook his head. "I don't know how to thank you."

"I'll put our stuff below," Zaun said.

Maria stopped him. "Before you do that, we'll need to remove the body."

"Body?" the two men said in unison.

Maria told them about Saunders and how he tried to have his way with her.

"Unbelievable," Zaun said.

"Wow," Jack said, running a hand over his chin. "I'm so glad you're okay. I never would've thought to check the cabin."

"Now do you see why we should stick together?" Zaun asked.

"Yeah, yeah," Jack said and shoved Zaun toward the cabin. "Let's get that body overboard."

"I'll help," Maria said.

"No," Jack told her. "We got this." He knew Maria was more than capable of doing the chore, but didn't think she should have to look at, let alone, touch the scumbag's corpse.

Zaun went down to the cabin first and stopped at the doorway. "Um," he said. "I think we have a problem."

"What is it?" Jack asked.

"Boats filling up with water."

"What?" Maria shouted.

"And there's a lot of it."

Jack remembered how Maria's boat sat lower in the water than the one he and Zaun had been on.

"Damn it," Maria said, stomping the deck. "The asshole's gun went off during our struggle. Bullet must have punctured a hole in the floor."

Jack squeezed passed Zaun on the stairs. The cabin was a bathtub, the dead body visible at the bottom. He turned around and went topside. "We need to get to shore. Boat's finished."

Cursing under her breath, Maria steered the boat to the nearest shore, about a quarter mile south of the Tappan Zee Bridge's southern side. The beach was heavily weeded, but the frigid temperature made the ground rock-hard. A steep, snow-covered incline led up to the Thruway. Jack knew the area somewhat from his many trips to his sister's house before the "incident." The Thruway was a highway that extended from Yonkers to Albany, then on to the Buffalo area and veering across the state to Pennsylvania.

"What now?" Zaun asked, climbing out of the boat.

The immediate answer was to get to the Thruway, then follow it to Cornwall, but it would never be that simple. They were in a heavily trafficked area. During rush hour, the bridge and about ten miles of road after it was always congested. People having fled from the city and the Westchester area after the epidemic would have made the road a parking lot. Jack feared there would be a lot of undead roaming around, but without a boat, what choice did they have but to cross the bridge?

"We go up," Jack said. "The highway is just over this hill. I'll check it out."

Zaun and Maria waited by the boat while Jack climbed, the snow making the task slick in places. When he reached the top, a four-foot tall cement divider wall extended to the left for about 200 feet, and to the right where it met the New York State Bridge and Tunnel building. He crept up to the wall and peered over it. Just as he thought, a line of cars extended in both directions—down the road toward the city and over the bridge. A few undead meandered about. All those abandoned vehicles, he thought. Where the hell did all the people go?

Sudden movement from Jack's right caught his attention. A lone zombie had spotted him and was heading his way. "Shit," he muttered and scrambled back down the incline.

"Roadway's clogged with abandoned vehicles," he said. "Both the north and south bound lanes have north bound traffic. Guess there wasn't much desire to head south. Oh, and there's undead. One spotted me. I think it's best if—" a scraping sound from above caught Jack's attention.

A zombie fell over the wall, then tumbled down the hill. Jack and the others hurried out of its way. The thing crashed into the boat, then began to rise. Without hesitation, Zaun stepped up and sank his sword into its skull.

More undead were falling over the barricade. The damn thing wasn't high enough to stop the undead.

"We have to move," Maria said.

They ran north along the shoreline. Jack glanced over his shoulder and saw a number of zombies tumbling down the hill, while others were already at the bottom and heading after them. He and the others rounded a bend and lost sight of the undead.

They reached the ten-foot-high, razor-wire-topped fence that ran up the hill, preventing anyone access to the bridge's underbelly.

"We're going to have to climb the hill," Jack said.

"Up there?" Zaun pointed. "Are you nuts?"

"We stay here," Maria said, "and we'll be overrun with undead. Maybe the bridge isn't too badly infested with the things."

The incline was steep. Jack didn't think the zombies would be able to climb it. "We can go up halfway and wait. See how many undead are coming our way. Maybe only a small number were attracted to us. We can take them out, then head back down the shore, or try to find something to cut our way through the fence. I'm afraid that with all the abandoned vehicles up there, the number of undead will be huge."

They went up about forty feet before finding a place to stop. Within minutes, a mass of at least fifty bot-controlled corpses came ambling along the shoreline. They collided with the fence and crammed into each other like the mindless things they were.

There were too many to kill by sword, and shooting them would severely lessen their ammo supply and attract more undead.

Maria tapped Jack on the shoulder and whispered, "Looks like they don't know we're up here."

"All right," Zaun said, "let's keep going then." He took a step and slipped, landing on his face.

Maria covered her mouth, holding back a laugh.

Jack smiled, and couldn't believe how damn funny that was, even in the terrible situation they were in.

Zaun pushed himself up. "Very—" and then his foot flew out from under him.

Jack saw his friend fall backwards. He reached out a hand to grab him, but he was too late. Zaun tumbled backwards down the hill.

CHAPTER 4

Jack and Maria rushed down the hill, watching as Zaun crashed into the horde of undead, knocking a small number of them down and into the water.

Zaun was up in minutes, but the undead were on him. Grimy, rotting hands latched onto him like the jaws of a Pit Bull. He twisted and turned, trying to give himself room, then kicked and punched. A zombie got through his assault and chomped down on his shoulder, tearing away a piece of his coat. Another was grabbing at his right leg. He pulled his sword out and sliced the thing's arms off as it attempted to bite him. The undead things were relentless. They showed no fear, no excitement. Not a single emotion was written on their faces to match their eager desire for human flesh.

Jack landed a blow with his feet into the side of a heavy-set zombie, knocking it into three others and sending them all to the ground. He pulled his Sig Sauer and began plugging the nearest undead. Maria was next to him doing the same with her Glock. Zaun continued to hack and slash. A small undead child snuck through the mass and latched onto his leg. Another zombie was about to grab him from behind, but Maria put a slug into its head.

"We need to get the hell out of here," Jack hollered, stating the obvious as he glanced down the shoreline. A line of undead were coming and would soon add to the throng.

Zaun cried out. Jack saw the undead kid, its teeth buried into Zaun's leg like a ravenous tick. Jack continued to shoot the nearest undead, dropping them like flies, but there were so many. Too many. He saw Maria reloading. Zaun pried off the undead kid, shoving it back into the crowd. He swung wide, slicing off three zombie heads at the same time. Jack's gun clicked empty. Instead of reloading, he pulled his .45 and began plugging away.

"Let's go," Maria said, yanking on Zaun's collar. It looked like Zaun almost refused as he kept slicing and dicing arms and heads, but finally he turned around and followed Maria up the hill. Jack backpedaled, slipping as he tried to climb. He spun around and started up when one of the undead grabbed his foot. He kicked back hard, connecting with the thing, then got purchase and hauled his ass upward.

They made their way about twenty feet up before stopping, everyone breathing heavily. The dead below attempted to pursue, but only slid or tumbled back down.

"Shit," Maria said, "that was too close."

"Zaun," Jack said, "are you okay?"

"I don't know. I mean my leg hurts." He fiddled with the pant leg and saw that it was ripped, the flesh below bleeding. "Damn, the little bitch bit me."

"We better take care of that now," Maria said. She removed her pack and took out her taser. Zaun found an area where he could lay. Jack positioned himself on the hill right below Zaun, ready to catch him should he slide.

Zaun pulled up his shirt. "Okay, do it."

Maria aimed and fired two darts into his abdominal area. Zaun's body trembled as the current traveled through it. Finished, Maria loaded another charge into the weapon. Zaun pulled out the darts and tossed them aside.

"Hit me again. Just to be sure."

"Oh, I was going to. Don't you worry," she said, then reloaded the gun and shot him again.

Finished, she reloaded the taser and returned it to her pack.

One 50,000-volt jolt had been enough, until they found a soldier who had obviously been tasered but still turned. Reynolds had said the bots were adapting and would grow stronger. Maybe one 50,000 volt shot wasn't enough anymore, so it was wise to give a person a double dose of electricity.

The group rested for a few minutes, drank some water and ate a little of the food they had. Below, the undead mass swelled, more having joined the ones already there. With all the gunfire, Jack had worried more undead would come spilling over the hill above them, but that didn't prove to be the case.

Ready to roll, they headed up the hill to where the land flattened out into a small ledge and a ten-foot chain-link fence topped with barbed wire stood, separating the roadway and bridge access from them. Jack didn't see any undead and was grateful.

They made their way along the fence to where it ended at the side of the Thruway Authority building. A number of windows stood about six feet from the ground. All were covered by a mesh grate except for one, which was on the ground along with broken glass.

"We go in, then make our way out the front," Jack whispered. "Easier than trying to go around the side of the building and having to cut through the fence."

Maria nodded.

She removed her pack. Jack and Zaun helped her up so she could take a look inside. "It's a bathroom. The stench is awful, but it's clear. I'm going in."

Zaun and Jack followed, Jack tossing in the bags before Zaun pulled him up.

Maria was right; the place smelled horrible with a mixture of feces, piss and blood, a lot of blood.

"I think I'm going to be sick," Zaun said.

"Breathe through your mouth," Maria told him.

Jack went over to the restroom's door. He cracked it open, listened, then opened the door to a narrow hallway; the walls were painted a light green. Smears of red extended in both directions. He waved to the others to follow.

He went left, hoping he was heading toward the front of the building and possibly a way out. He passed a closed door on his right, then came to an open one. Peering inside, he saw a paper-strewn desk with a computer monitor, posters of the bridge on the walls and a zombie in the far corner. It appeared to have been a middle-aged man. The thing was wearing a Thruway Authority uniform, its right hand a grisly stump of exposed bone and flesh. It faced away from Jack, standing still. He had seen this behavior before—a zombie settled in one place when there was no action or place to roam. It had probably been trapped inside the building for so long without prey, and simply stopped moving, possibly saving its energy.

Jack turned his head, motioning for Zaun.

Zaun came forward, sword already drawn. He entered the room and pierced the zombie's head without it even knowing he was there. He wiped the blade off on a jacket hanging on a coat rack before sheathing his sword.

A scuffling noise from down the hall caused Jack to take his eyes from the room. Another Thruway-Authority zombie was coming their way. This one was female with long blonde hair. Jack motioned for Zaun who came from the room, saw the zombie, and severed its head in one fluid motion.

"Might as well keep that puppy out," Maria said, indicating Zaun's samurai sword.

They continued down the hall, Zaun in the lead, and came to a large welcome area. A reception counter took up the far wall. A waiting room with multiple chairs took up the opposite corner. An empty water cooler rested next to one of the chairs. Three dead bodies lay on the floor, the corpses nothing more than bone.

The place was a mess with papers lying about, coffee cups, soda cans, a vending machine was overturned—the large glass window smashed out. Not even a wrapper left inside. The acrid stench of rot was thick here. Jack pulled his jacket up over his nose.

"No way we're staying here," Maria said.

Jack went over to the front doors. The glass was frosted, making it impossible to see outside. He undid the lock, then opened the door and poked his head out. He had a clear view of the roadway in both directions. Hundreds of parked cars lined the lanes, bumper to bumper.

He stepped out and didn't see any movement, save an American flag blowing in the wind, tied to the end of a station wagon's antennae. But with all the vehicles, especially the big rigs and their trailers, it made it difficult to get an unobstructed view of much in either direction. A zombie could be meandering between vehicles right ahead of him and he wouldn't know it. Hopefully, the undead that were in the area had tumbled down the hill earlier and were now trapped there—but with so many vehicles about, he doubted it.

A zombie staggered from around a box truck. It was about one hundred feet away. One was no problem. Then he saw another bot-controlled corpse appear from behind a car. Okay, a couple, even a small group, they could handle, even outrun them if they had to.

Turning around, he saw Maria's head poking from the partially open door and waved her out. Zaun followed with sword in hand and took the lead.

They walked single file. No one spoke. Taps on the shoulder and pointing were the methods of communicating. A few of the undead were on their trail as well as in front of them. Zaun would take them out as they neared. Keeping the noise down and ammo saved were priority numbers one and two.

They mostly passed by abandoned cars and trucks. The few with undead inside them were left alone, the mindless corpses unable to get out of the vehicles.

There were a number of fender benders and a couple of accidents. A pickup truck had run up and onto a small car. A woman hung out of a Volkswagen, the flesh all but gone from her skull. Jack cringed, wondering if she had been alive when the undead started eating her.

The going was slow. The small number of undead behind and ahead of them began to multiply quickly. More and more came from hidden places. They didn't groan or sigh, but they made plenty of noise, banging into cars and falling over dead bodies.

By the time they were halfway across the bridge, about thirty undead were on their trail. Zaun had sliced a few heads off of the ones that were in the way, but now with the number so large and gaining, he switched to his M4 rifle.

Jack and the others used controlled bursts to take out the closest undead, but the damn things seemed to be multiplying as more and more came at them. Heads exploded, painting vehicles with brain and skull fragments. Jack felt like he was back in the city, when they were trying to reach the warehouse. There had been so many undead closing in on them. But there, they had a place to run to and more room to do it in. Here, they were boxed in. Movement was difficult. The vehicles weren't all neatly lined up. Most were crooked, blocking off lanes, forcing the survivors to have to climb over them. The wind on the bridge was fierce and frigid.

"Reloading," Maria yelled and Jack took up covering her side. They were walking past a tractor-trailer. Jack was occupied with shooting an undead woman who reached out of a car window at him when something grabbed his ankle. He jerked his foot and looked down to see a legless zombie pawing at him. He kicked it in the face, dislocating its jaw. There were other undead crawling toward him from farther back.

"Under the rig. There's more under the rig."

Zaun and Maria were too busy firing at the approaching mass. Jack pulled his .45 and began plugging the prone zombies in the head. One made it to Zaun and latched onto his boot. Jack went to warn him, but the agile martial artist pulled his leg back, then stomped on the thing's head, crushing it into a pile of mush.

"We have to move!" Jack yelled, holstering the .45, then taking aim with the M4.

With the number of undead ahead of them, it was almost impossible to move quickly. They blew brains out of heads and trudged forward. The bot-controlled corpses fell, but with so many undead the throng drew nearer.

"Slow and steady—" Jack began, but lost his ability to speak. His mouth fell open at the site ahead of him, and he did all he could to keep breathing.

CHAPTER 5

About three quarters of the way across the bridge, Jack couldn't think about anything but his imminent death. At the end of the bridge was what had to be a twenty-foot-high wall of stacked cars blocking their path. Now he understood why there were so many zombies on this side of the bridge—the damn things couldn't get across it. There was no way they could fight their way back. Jumping off wasn't an option either. If they survived the fall, they'd still have the icy waters to deal with, which would surely do them in.

"What the hell is that?" Zaun asked, staring at the wall.

Jack came out of his stupor and began firing at the approaching undead. "Just keep going. We'll figure it out."

"Damn it," Maria shouted, seeing the site. "We just can't catch a break!"

They continued to fire, concentrating more on taking out the undead ahead of them. As slow as the zombies were, the ones behind were getting closer. They needed to move faster. If they had any chance at climbing the wall of cars, they'd need time.

"Jack," Maria said, "are you seeing what I'm seeing?"

Jack took his eyes from the zombie he'd just sent down and eyed the wall. Three figures stood atop it. By the way they moved and the guns they held, they weren't undead. Now they just had to see if they were friendlies. One of the figures threw something sparkly onto the bridge near a small grouping of undead.

"Get down!" Jack yelled. A second later, he heard and felt the explosion. Peering over the car he had ducked behind, he saw that the group of undead were gone. Arms, legs and other body parts flew in all directions. One zombie remained mostly whole and landed on the roof of a Ford Escape, blowing out the rear window.

Jack watched as another ignited stick of explosive landed at the feet of a few approaching zombies. A moment later, the threesome was down, their legs blown off. Shrapnel from one of the vehicles flew past his head. More dynamite was tossed, obliterating more undead ahead, clearing a path to the wall.

"I hope they're trying to help us and not lure us in for a kill," Zaun shouted.

"If we don't keep moving, it won't matter," Maria said.

Jack could smell the stench of rot from the approaching horde. He could no longer hear them banging into the side of vehicles or falling over each other as they hurried forward—the explosions causing a ringing in his ears.

As they drew near to the wall, the figures stopped tossing dynamite. Jack and the others were able to hoof it, somewhat distancing themselves from the zombies.

"Move your asses!" one of the people on the wall yelled.

Only a few undead were left ahead of them. Jack took two out, Zaun and Maria the rest. As they approached the wall, a rope ladder was let down.

Jack told Zaun to go up first, thinking if there was a problem, the guy could handle the strangers at close range. Maria went up next, then Jack, who scrambled up the ladder just as the first of the undead approached the wall.

"Thanks," Jack said, breathing hard. He stood and shook the hand of an older man. The guy wore a baseball cap, wire-rim glasses, and a bulky winter coat.

"Name's Don. We can share pleasantries once we get off of here." He motioned for Jack to go ahead. Zaun and Maria were already on their way down from the wall, stepping on the roofs of a descending line of vehicles, like giant stairs.

From atop the wall, Jack could see, for about a quarter mile out, that the highway was clear of vehicles—save an armored truck parked a few feet away—and then the parking lot started up again.

"You're not the first to try crossing the bridge," Don said, looking from Jack to Maria to Zaun. "You must have a good reason for doing so."

Jack nodded. "Trying to get to my sister."

"Where's she from?"

"Cornwall."

"That's a ways off—by foot anyways."

"Hi, I'm Zaun," Zaun said, stepping up to shake Don's hand.

"Good to meet you all," Don said.

"Maria," Maria said.

Don motioned to a tall, lanky, young man with acne. "This here's Rob." The kid waved and said hello. "And this fellow on my left is—"

"Paul," the man said. He was holding a .30-06 semi-automatic rifle with a banana clip. He had a full beard and soft eyes. "You guys military?"

"No," Zaun said. "Well, she is," he poked a thumb in Maria's direction, "or rather was. Not sure we have one anymore."

"Tell that to the fighter planes we saw flying overhead the other day," Don said. "Not sure how together they are, but some kind of military is still around."

"Probably using Stewart Air Force Base in Newburgh," Maria said.

"That's near Cornwall," Jack added, speaking specifically to Maria. "Maybe you'll be able to hitch a ride south."

"Yeah, right," she said.

"Anyway," Don said, "we should head in. You're welcome to join us, and I'd suggest it. Looks like we got bad weather coming in; temperature's going to drop."

Jack noticed the kid looking around, off into the distance. He was wary about something. Jack eyed Maria, who noticed it too.

"Something wrong?" Jack asked.

"It isn't exactly safe around here," Don said. "And I'm not talking about the undead, though in recent days it's safer around here than it was after the dead started rising. It's a good idea not to be out in the open."

"Do you know what's over there?" Paul asked, pointing across the water.

"Tarrytown, then Ossining—home to Sing Sing Prison," Zaun answered.

"That's right," Paul said. "Never thought we'd have to deal with *that* all the way over here, but trouble has a way of surviving, and finding those that don't want it."

"So you've had problems with the inmates?" Jack asked. "Have a few made their way over here?"

Don laughed. "A few? Try a whole bunch."

"A cell block's worth," Paul spat.

"Can we go now?" Rob asked. "It isn't like those explosions weren't hard to hear."

As if on cue, two zombies, both naked from the waist down, came stumbling out of the nearby tree line.

"Damn things are everywhere," Paul said. He aimed his rifle and blew the head off of one zombie, then fired again and turned its partner's head to mist.

"Time to leave," Don said. "You people coming?"

Jack looked at the others. He saw the tiredness on their faces.

Maria nodded.

Zaun shrugged. "Why not . . ."

"Sounds good, Don," Jack said. "We have our own food. Just need a place to rest up."

"Nonsense," the man said, waving his arm, "we've got plenty to eat and drink. You'll need your food for the long journey ahead."

"That's very kind of you," Maria said.

"Alrighty then," Don said, "come with us."

They headed to the armored car. Rob opened the rear doors and climbed in. Jack, Maria and Zaun all stopped, their faces wary.

Don laughed. "You can all ride up front with me if it'll make you feel better. Paul and Rob will ride in the back."

Jack and Maria got in the front with Don while Zaun decided to ride in the back.

Not only was the truck bulletproof, but it was also zombie proof. Anything undead in the way would be flattened. The feeling of security it brought was immeasurable.

"So, before you said it wasn't safe to be out, but was safer than it used to be?" Maria asked.

Don nodded as he drove the truck away. A necklace with a butterfly emblem swayed from the overhead visor.

"After the shit hit the fan, so to speak, a bunch of people from the area settled into a large house up on the hill. We call it Cliff House. We organized ourselves, gathered weapons, food and other supplies. We thought we'd wait out whatever was happening

27

together. The military had blocked off the bridge using those bulldozers you saw. They killed anyone trying to come over it. Guess they thought they could contain the problem, or at least keep it from spreading quicker." Don wiped his forehead with the back of his hand.

"Anyway . . . before that happened, a bunch of inmates had already gotten over the bridge. Don't know why they headed this way, but they did. They took residence in a mansion about six or seven miles from here. They went around killing, raping and pillaging, like some barbarian-order out of a fantasy novel. The ones they didn't kill were taken to the mansion, to their leader, a monster named Cannibal. A vile human, if I ever saw one."

Don shifted gears, picking up speed.

"When they came at us, we were ready and fought them off, but lost two of our own in the process. We managed to capture one of theirs—that's how we know so much about them and their psycho leader, Cannibal."

"Where's the prisoner now?" Jack asked.

Don stared ahead. "Gone."

Silence filled the cab. Don turned the truck off the highway and drove through the busted metal guardrail, and headed up a snowy incline to a double-yellow lined road that led into the mountains.

"We don't have weapons like yours, but we got plenty of rifles, shotguns and handguns. As long as we keep on our toes, we'll be able to fight off those scumbags should they try attacking us again, though I think they might've moved on."

"Moved on?" Maria asked. "Scum like that don't usually move on."

"After the third time they tried attacking us, we killed four of their men. It's been three weeks since we heard anything from them, let alone anyone else. I think we proved to be too much trouble. They probably moved on and are terrorizing some other folks. I don't like it, but it ain't like we're going to chase after them. We've fortified and dug in. The whole world looks like it's gone to Hell and we're not about to join it."

Jack bounced around as the truck rolled over a few downed tree branches.

"Good for you," Maria said.

"This is our home. Most of us are from the area. We have no idea what the rest of the state, let alone country is like. Figured we'd wait and see what happens. In the meantime, we've got guns, the river for fishing, and wildlife to help sustain us, along with canned food. The house is in a great location—and I'm not talking about the view."

They passed by a number of small roads with names like, Maple Way, Cranberry Lane, and Willy Creek Road. They came to an intersection and Don took the truck left onto Fairview Street. The woods were thick here. Jack looked out the side window and could no longer see the bridge. It seemed as if they'd entered another world, a snow-covered winter wonderland where trouble wasn't permitted to exist. Jack wished his mind would allow him to forget what was going on, but that wasn't possible. At least not now. Maybe tonight, when he was lying on a bed, he would be able to dream about the past and the good times. About his wife.

"What about a boat?" Maria said, bringing Jack back to the present.

"We've got row and canoe," Don said. "As you can imagine, when the outbreak made the news, people panicked. Anyone with a boat packed up and got the hell out of here. It's not like we're that far from the city. But I guess the military didn't want people scattering. A few fighter jets and Apaches flew up the river, destroying docks and marinas along the way, like the one back down by the bridge. Damnedest thing I ever saw. Stopping your own people from escaping."

Maria sighed. "They must've thought they could contain or at least slow the spread, but once it left the city, I don't see how it could have been contained."

"We heard reports about people being sick as far as California," Don said. "All it takes is one person on a plane I guess. Power went out soon after that story broke. Not sure if they nipped it in the bud or what. The Canadian border was cut off, bunch of tanks and helicopters set along it. But if Manhattan was quarantined and the sickness found its way out of there, then I'd say it'll get anywhere it wants."

"You're right about that," Jack agreed.

Don slowed the truck and took a left off the road and onto a narrow driveway. Huge trees, pines, leafless maples and oaks overhung the drive, creating the sensation of entering a tunnel.

"Well, we're here," Don said, pulling up to a yellow school bus. It was positioned sideways, blocking the path. Unlike a normal school bus, this one's windows and wheels were covered over with what appeared to be sheet metal.

The bus came to life and drove forward, giving the armored truck room to pass by.

The driveway opened up to a small clearing in the middle of the woods. A three story, three-car garage, monster-of-a-house stood at the center. The house's larger windows were covered over with something—sheets of plywood maybe? A man wearing sunglasses and a black winter hat was on the roof, standing behind a makeshift barrier. He held a rifle in his hands. A pickup truck, two SUVs, and another armored car, identical to the one that Jack was in, were sitting just off the driveway. Movement to his right caught his attention. A gunman came from the woods. He held up a hand and waved.

Don returned the friendly gesture and killed the engine. "Home sweet home," he said, then opened the door. "Let's go meet everyone."

Jack and Maria exited the passenger side. Zaun was already outside. Jack looked back and saw that the school bus was blocking the driveway again. For the first time in a while, Jack felt safe.

He and the others were shown to their room for the night. It was small, but had three beds. The house was heated by two fireplaces, one at either end of the abode, but if the nights grew too cold, they were welcome to use a kerosene heater or sleep in the living room. They left their M4s and backpacks in the room, carrying their sidearms and knives with them.

Jack and the others were introduced to various residents as they made their way through the house. They finally ended up back in the living room, a fire blazing in the hearth. The heat was a blessing if there ever was one, Jack thought.

"This is my wife, Marcy," Don said. The woman smiled warmly and said hello.

Everyone introduced himself or herself before taking seats. Don sat next to his wife.

There were three others sitting around the fireplace. First, there was Paul whom they met earlier by the bridge. Jack and the others learned that Paul was a former construction worker and avid hunter. Sitting next to Paul was Duane, a forty-nine-year old trucker from New Jersey. Duane had made his way across the bridge and got stuck in traffic on the other side. He remained in his truck for two days until a group of people found him. "I saw Don and some others and figured it was my only chance, so I made a run for it. They saved my bacon." Then there was Tony, a forty-year-old with three kids. His wife, Heather, died three weeks ago from the contagion.

Jack, Maria and Zaun told their harrowing tale of how they were at the heart of the outbreak and fought their way out of the bunker and the city. Jack made sure to tell them about the bots and how the dead were being controlled by them, then adding how bites were curable.

"Damn, that's some story," Duane said.

"Curable?" Tony asked, stunned. "Fucking curable? I could've saved my wife? And the fucking military knew?"

"Tony," Don said, "these are guests."

"It's okay," Jack said. "I lost my wife the same way. The people responsible for the contagion reached me too late. My wife was already dead. She was one of the first to become infected."

"You," Tony said, standing and pointing a finger at Maria. "You were part of this shit?"

Paul grabbed onto Tony. "Calm down."

"No," he hollered. "Fuck that." He stared at Maria, his face in a snarl. "Why didn't you people warn us? Warn everyone?" Tears were streaming down the man's face.

"Maria had no part in it," Jack said. "She had no idea what was going on in that hell hole. None of us did, and by the time we found out Manhattan was overrun, shut down, we were stuck five stories below ground and in the hands of a madman."

Silence followed Jack's statement. Looks of disbelief and sorrow spread across everyone's faces.

"So what now?" Don asked. "We don't have tasers to cure whoever might become infected."

"Best guess is to use a car battery. Rig it up so the voltage is 50,000. Maybe a little more. And make sure you shock the person twice, just to be certain you've killed all the little shits. Last info we received, the things were able to adapt, getting more resistant to electricity. Maybe it'll stay easy to kill them, maybe it won't."

Tony had his head in his hands, bent over. "So many people could've been saved if only the government didn't have their heads in their asses. My wife . . ." He rose to his feet and stormed out of the room.

"Tony's had it hard," Duane said. "We all have, but he's got little kids who no longer have a mother."

"It's been tough on us all," Don said. "I don't know a single person who hasn't lost someone."

"So," Marcy said, "where are you all heading?"

"To my sister's house," Jack said. "I don't know why, but I believe she's alive."

Marcy gave a nod, smiling.

"Once Jack gets to Cornwall," Maria said, "I'll be heading to North Carolina. My little girl's there with her uncle and grandmother."

"Well, we're glad to have you," Marcy said, "even if it's just for the night. You rest up, eat, and you'll be that much stronger for your journey."

"Thanks," Maria said.

"Yeah," Zaun echoed, "your hospitality and saving our butts is much appreciated."

Later that evening, just before dark, they ate dinner. The meal was incredible; freshly cooked Striped bass caught from the Hudson River, rice, baked beans, canned carrots, a variety of sodas, and wine. People seemed in good spirits, but tired and haggard. Jack understood and thought he and his friends fit in well. Looking around, his gut grew warm with a sense of hope. It was small, like an ember, but it was there and it gave him a boost of strength that he would find Sara. Even through terrible events like this undead phenomenon, people found a way to not only survive, but also come together.

Fuel had been gathered from surrounding gas stations and vehicles, including things like lawnmowers. The generators were used sparingly to run the house's lights when needed, the pumps for the well, and the tools for fixing things or fortifying them. During the warmer months, should the undead situation last that long, they would need the generators to run the refrigerators and freezers, but for now, the winter and snow kept the fish and deer meat from spoiling.

When it was time for bed, Jack and the others thought it was best to be vigilant and slept in shifts like they had back in the city. As much as Don and his people seemed like nice, caring people, they couldn't take a chance that there was a bad seed or two among them. It was better to be prepared.

The night went without a hitch, everyone slept well. They ate a hearty breakfast and were given some deer meat to take with them.

"Well," Don said, "I wish you all could stay, but I understand that family comes first. I hope you find your sister, Jack, and you your daughter, Maria."

"Thank you, Don," Maria said, shaking his hand. "You have something good here. Keep protecting it."

"Stick to the roads I showed you on the map. Then, when you get to the Thruway, follow it all the way to Harriman, then take route 32 to Cornwall. You'll have about a quarter mile of clear highway before the cars start clogging up the road again. Not sure what you'll find up there, but if I had to bet on anyone knowing how to take care of themselves, it'd be you all."

Jack and the others thanked Don again, waved to the people standing on the deck, and headed down the driveway.

CHAPTER 6

Jack and the others headed along the mountain road. He hoped the trip would go smoothly, but then thought about it and realized he was only deluding himself. Every step brought with it the fear of seeing a zombie. He and the others needed to be on their toes, but not so much that their anxiety wore them out. And after meeting the people of Cliff House, he now had to worry about the human element, the survivors who thrived in a lawless land. The true scum of the Earth. He hoped to run into more people like Don and Paul.

It started to snow. Large, puffy flakes like feathers from a burst pillow, were falling dreamily to the ground. The scene was beautiful, serene. Jack shivered as a flake landed on the back of his neck, sneaking through his upturned collar, but he welcomed it. This was a great distraction. Something only nature could provide. An illusion to what was really going on. Jack felt himself let go a little. He looked around, wondering if maybe things were going to get better. Be easier. This sudden scene of beauty was almost overwhelming.

He watched the others for a moment and how they walked with determination. They were on guard, ready for action. Jack needed this reprieve, if only for a few minutes. He forgot about the killing and the undead. This was his time. Time to heal a little. Let nature have its way with him. Show him that the world still had beauty, and that there was something stunning in the wake of so much horribleness. In the long run, the snow could mean more problems for them, but for now, he was living in the moment. Tomorrow might not be here. Things in life were never guaranteed, but they were even less so currently.

Jack looked around, trying hard to absorb what he saw. He would hold onto the images and use them as reminders of how wonderful the world was. Add enough of them together and he could have a happy place to return to when the going got really tough, when the heaviness in his heart felt like it was too much to bear.

"Sure is quiet," Zaun said.

Jack felt as if he'd been smacked back to reality. His small vacation had been great, but he suddenly realized how dangerous that was to do. He'd just been telling himself how he and the others needed to remain on guard. He'd practically allowed himself to sleepwalk.

"That's what happens when you spend your whole life in the city," Jack said. "Nature becomes an oddity when it should really be the other way around."

"I like it," Zaun said, "but I could use a car horn or siren once in awhile."

"Reminds me of home," Maria said. "The woods, that is. I'll take peace and quiet and even the cold over what we went through."

The temperature was bitter, but they were dressed for the weather and had each other. Nothing was discussed as to where they would spend the night. Jack supposed it would be some abandoned house along the way. There had to be a lot of them. Maybe they'd even find a vehicle and a stretch of highway that wasn't congested and make Cornwall tonight. There he went again, thinking things would be easy. Realistically, the best scenario would have them arriving in two or three days depending on the weather, and if the roadway was clogged all the way to Harriman, then they'd be walking the entire way.

Jack hadn't spent much time imagining his sister not being home. But what if she wasn't there? If he was being honest with himself—there was a good chance she wouldn't be. She'd have most likely gone to a place where people were able to hole up. A place like Cliff House. How would he ever find her if that was the case?

Then there was the really awful scenario. The one he didn't want to acknowledge. Couldn't imagine. What if his sister was . . . dead?

Jack's legs grew heavy.

He looked to Maria and Zaun as they walked a little ahead of him. He had let his mind wander, and that was a bad idea. His sister was alive. There was no need to think otherwise—at least not now. He needed a reason to carry on. He was still grieving his wife and wasn't about to add his sister to the list. As far as he was concerned, she was alive.

Sara was a smart woman. She had always been level-headed, did well in school, and had a strong heart. Growing up together, she was always supportive of Jack. She looked out for him, covered for him and loved spending time with him. She was the most loving, caring person he knew. Along with that, she was also tough. She never let others influence her. In eleventh grade, her boyfriend had wanted her to come trick or treating. He and most of her friends were going to spray-paint the outside of the high school. She refused to be a part of it. They were never caught and it was a night they all said they'd never forget, but Sara was okay with that. She was happy with her decision. He was so proud of her when he found out.

Jack shook his head, frustrated; because as grounded as his sister was, as book-smart and street-smart as she proved to be, how the hell did she wind up with her asshole husband?

Jack had been to a number of parties where the guy got plastered and became a jerk. Sara said it was only when he drank too much, which wasn't often. Then, after they were married, the real monster came out—drunk or not. How could she stay with him? Marriage was a serious matter, but when you were with a man who drank too much, refused counseling, and hit his wife, it was time to leave. And they didn't have kids, so using them as the reason for staying wasn't applicable.

During his last visit to her house, the asshole had gotten drunk and threatened Sara. Jack had enough and beat the shit out of him. Sara called the cops and Jack spent the night in jail. After that, he was done with her. He cut himself off. A year had gone by with no communication between them. He couldn't figure out how he and

Sara had become so distant. Life was so damn complicated at times. It was impossible for him to wrap his head around how a woman like Sara could become a victim of abuse, a stranger to all that knew her. But as time went on, he realized why she had acted so. She was a victim of abuse. Worn down by a monster. She'd lost who she was, or was on her way to doing so. Jack had abandoned her when she needed him most. He ground his teeth, wishing he'd been there for her.

Dwelling on it now wasn't going to do anything except fuel his anger. Yeah, the guy had Jack thrown in jail, and yeah, Sara backed her lying husband, but still it was obvious she needed help and was scared to be alone with him.

Jack swore to himself that when he found her, he'd never let her down again.

CHAPTER 7

Cable stood just off the road, his large frame hidden between two trees sharing a base. He peered through the scope on his Browning 300, waiting for the targets to enter his field of view. He was a crack shot. His years in the military had honed his natural ability; shoot to kill. Whether quietly from long range or up close and personal, he was proficient at both.

He saw the three companions, then focused on each of their faces, stopping on the woman's. He did a double take, thinking he saw a ghost. But it wasn't a ghost, because there were no such things. Then again, there were no such things as zombies either, yet they were everywhere.

Damn, the woman was a spitting image of his ex-wife, his beautiful ex-wife. As he watched the female draw nearer to his position, his mind wandered to the past.

During his youth, he ran with a local gang, got into trouble and almost ruined his life. His father, a mean drunk, but caring when he was sober, got him to join the military after he graduated high school.

The army had straightened him out and had shown him a different side of life. And as much as he hated his father, he loved the man the same. If it hadn't been for him, he wasn't sure he'd be alive today.

Cable's first tour of duty was in Afghanistan. It was only supposed to be one and done, but like so many others, he did three. The shit he'd done and seen while over there was impossible to forget. It built up within him, like an over-inflated inner tube. He was ready to burst at the end of the third go round, but was sent home for good just in time. The constant stress of combat, of not knowing who to trust, was overwhelming. But he didn't complain. He performed his duties, keeping the pain down deep.

His dreams were filled with the images that had been seared into his brain; dead men, women and children, their bodies dismembered and shredded from bullets or explosives. One of the most reoccurring dreams was when he slipped and fell face first onto a bloody, semi-charred corpse. His mouth had been open, the guts sloshing into it. No matter how much he cleansed his palate, he still tasted the cadaver's flesh. He'd seen a young boy carrying a basket of fruit get his head blown off by a gunman, the fruit cascading to the ground like trash. People ran for cover, but when the gunman was killed, they came from their houses and gathered the fruit, and then ran off.

When it was time to go home, he was beyond relieved. His life would never be normal. He knew what he had done and the things he had seen had changed him forever. But that was true for any soldier, and he had a wonderful wife and daughter to go home to. To love.

To his dismay, life stateside wasn't great. His wife was distant. Maybe it was her having to work overtime most days. His military pension was decent, but sitting around all day wasn't something he enjoyed. He needed to work.

Trying to find a job proved difficult. He'd thought his former military status would give him a leg up, and it did, but only in places where he was qualified. Fast food, gas stations, and department stores. He'd put his life on the line, fought for his country, and this was what his country had to offer him?

His wife's hours were cut back only a few days after she found out that she was pregnant. They'd only had sex a few times since he had been home. He was glad his swimmers were still in top form. But now the bills were coming in and not getting paid in full like they had been. And once the new child came, things were only going to get tighter.

"You need to get a job," Leela demanded. "You can't sit around and mope. Something is better than nothing." She threw a stained kitchen towel at him. "Soon, that'll be a baby's diaper. Remember? We have a kid on the way. You want your kid to starve?"

As usual, he held in his need to scream at her, to scream in general. Absorb the tension, let the body dissipate it.

He hooked up with some childhood friends a few days later. It surprised him to see that some of them were still alive, and didn't surprise him to see that others had died. They were making money, living large. Nice cars, jewelry and no worries about paying the bills.

"Come on," Jay said, "we could use a man with your expertise. No one gets hurt. Easy money."

He kept seeing his wife's angry face, his daughter going to school without new clothes, the new baby crying because it was hungry. He was probably making a bigger deal out of his thoughts than need be, but some quick cash until he got on his feet wouldn't hurt. He'd do this one job, then be done.

They knocked off a local meth lab, stealing $50,000 worth of the drug. His cut was two grand. No one had gotten hurt. The place had only one guard and he was taken out non-lethally, just as Jay had promised. Cable decided to stick around. The job situation wasn't going to improve anytime soon and the money was too good to pass up. "What and when is the next gig?" he asked Jay.

"We do it all, brother. Whatever someone wants, we get it done. We also do a little for ourselves."

Cable went on to steal cars for chop shops, broke into people's homes for their cash and valuables, and even slung a few bags of crack here and there.

It was during a cold November night that Cable's luck started to run out.

He'd been doing a home robbery—the family supposed to be out for the night— when he was surprised by one of the house's occupants. Cable threw the silhouetted figure to the ground. It was a young kid, maybe a teenager. The kid stared at him, then started screaming. "Help, help." Cable told him to shut up, that he'd be out of there fast. But the kid kept screaming. Cable saw red, envisioned the cops coming, the neighbors calling the police. His life would be over. If only the kid would shut up so he could do what he had to do. Before he realized it, he was on top of the kid, squeezing the life out of him. He heard a snapping sound, and the kid's eyes bulged from their sockets. "No, no, no," he shouted. "Wake up, wake up." He tried CPR but the kid was dead. He'd crushed his windpipe.

He started using drugs, taking from the shit he sold. The jobs became sloppier and Jay told him to get control of himself, then come back to him for work.

"I need the money, man," he pleaded. "Please, Jay."

"You killed a kid!" Jay said. "I get it. Shit happens. But damn, you're all fucked up. I know you're using. I can see it in your eyes. You're jittery and shit. You're a liability. Get yourself cleaned up and then come back to me."

Cable got on his hands and knees. "Please, man. I need work. I need cash. I'll kick this shit. Straighten myself out."

"You look pathetic, dog." Jay spat. "Get the fuck out of my sight before I put a bullet in your ass."

Cable felt something inside of him shut off. He went numb, the tears on his cheeks felt like ice water. He grabbed the knife from his belt and plunged it into Jay's gut. The man's eyes widened in disbelief. Cable got to his feet and cranked the knife, twisting it in deeper, grinding his teeth. He stared his old friend in the eyes. "You're just like the rest of them. Use me up, then toss me away."

Jay let out a squeak and collapsed to the floor. Cable brought the knife to his mouth and licked the blade clean. He'd done this before, in Afghanistan. He wasn't sure why, but it made him feel like a demon. Invincible. He cleaned out all the cash and drugs from Jay's stash.

He went out and got high, then decided it was a good idea to show his wife the bag of money he acquired, totaling just under $30,000. She'd be proud of him, he thought. Of course he'd leave out the killing, saying he earned the money playing cards—a one time thing.

She didn't believe him.

"Tell me where you got this money, Mathew," Leela demanded, staring at the bag of cash. "I'm not having stolen money in my home."

"It ain't like that—" he tried telling her.

"Bullshit it ain't like that," she shot back. "Someone, and not someone friendly, is going to come looking for that cash. Put that shit back and pray no one knows you took it."

"I earned this. It's ours."

She stepped up to him; glared into his eyes. "Are you fucking high?"

"What? No, baby." He went to touch her, but she batted his hand away.

"Don't fucking touch me," she told him, a look of utter disgust on her face. "You're on drugs . . . and show up with all this cash . . ." She shook her head.

"It's all good," he pleaded. "No one's going to come looking. I took care of it."

She shot him a cold look. "What do you mean, 'you took care of it'?"

"I mean nobody's going to come looking for this. It's ours."

She eyed the bag carefully. "Is that blood?"

"I cut myself, that's all."

"You repulse me," she spat. "Get the hell out of my house!" She picked up the bag and threw it at him. "And take your drug, blood money with you."

Rage burned inside his head. He'd done whatever he had to do to take care of his family, to provide, and now his wife was throwing him out? Making him feel small, useless. Pathetic.

"I should've divorced your ass years ago," she said, viciously. "You were a no good loser then and you're a no good loser now."

"Come on, baby," he said, holding back the need to scream. "You and Kyla are my world. And we got another on the way. Take the money. We can use this."

She smiled, but it wasn't warmly. "You sad sack of shit. Kyla isn't even yours. And neither is this one coming." She patted her stomach. "Had an affair when you were away. Would've left your ass too if he hadn't died. A fucking car accident of all things. So I just kept my mouth shut."

"You're just saying that."

"Really? You think that one time you were home you got me pregnant? That one, short, less than a minute romp you gave me? Got me a new man on the side who wants to marry me once I leave your ass. He can't have kids and loves mine."

Cable didn't understand where any of this was coming from. Yes, he knew things were tense between him and his wife, but not this. Not cheating. And wait, did she say his kids weren't his?

"Kyla isn't mine?"

"You stupid ass. You really are an idiot. That's what I said. So there's no need for you to be here or be in our lives. I want a divorce and I want your sorry, pathetic excuse for a life out of ours!"

The room went red. He'd experienced this before. It had happened overseas and when he was with that kid during the break-in. He lost control, became the demon. Before he knew it, he was on top of his wife, stabbing her in the gut, killing her and some other guy's baby. He stared into her eyes, knowing now what he truly was. He was a monster. A killer. "Fuck you, bitch."

She didn't die right away. He let her bleed out, but not before his daughter came home.

Cable welcomed the girl, opening his arms wide, bloody knife in his hand. She tried to run back out the door, but he caught her by her ponytail and yanked her back inside. She screamed for help, and he wrapped her up in a bear hug.

"Please . . ." his wife said, raising an arm toward him.

"You can have her," Cable said, and ran the blade across the girl's neck, then tossed her on top of her mother.

The police arrived ten minutes later, the neighbors hearing the screams. Cable was sitting in the kitchen eating cereal, the milk having reddened from the blood dripping off his hands.

When all was said and done, he was sentenced to life in prison. Knowing how to fight, being former military, and weighing over two-forty, all muscle, his time inside went without much of a problem. It was the boredom he hated. He needed to be commanded. To kill on the battlefield. He mostly sat alone in his cell, going back to the desert, back with his squad where he felt his best.

Then the world changed. The dead came back to life, and to make matters worse—they were hungry for human flesh.

Reminiscing on life, Cable could've imagined a lot of things, but a world-ending apocalypse wasn't one of them. The prison went into full lockdown. Guards weren't permitted to leave. That lasted about a day, and then the underpaid patrol officers scrammed, leaving the prison unguarded. A group of inmates freed themselves, opened the prison, and it was adios from there.

Now, in this new world, this world of death and mayhem, Cable was reborn. He was back in his soldier frame-of-mind, but times a hundred. There was no one enemy; everyone was an enemy. He was a killer, and needed to be. The demon inside was let loose, liberated to enjoy itself. But seeing so many people slaughtered, eaten alive, walking around mindless, had even pierced the demon's hide somewhat.

Cable was at his best when he was a soldier and working under the command of another. He enjoyed being part of a team. For now, that team was with Cannibal—a truly sick man—and his crew of former inmates. It felt good to be a soldier again, taking orders and doing what he did best—killing.

He slowed his breathing, feeling the excitement of battle closing in. The falling snow practically sizzled against his skin. His orders were to take the newcomers alive, but if he had to, he'd kill them all.

CHAPTER 8

The ugly man called Scars came down the stairs. He visited often, eyeing the women in the cage with delight as he licked his cracked lips and rubbed his crotch, but he never assaulted them, at least not in the basement. The women were nothing more than chickens in a pen waiting to be taken, never to be seen again.

Scars held a gun in one hand as he unlocked the cage. It was time for another woman to leave. Jill Hannigan, along with everyone else, backed away. The man grinned and pointed. "You," he said. "Come here." She shook her head and begged him to choose someone else. He stared at her with utter hatred, then told her he wasn't going to tell her twice.

The captives had seen the results of what happened when a person didn't obey. The last woman was yanked out of the cage and taken away by force, punched and kicked. The next day Scars came to the basement with a bucket and pulled out her severed head, holding it by the blood-matted hair. "This is what happens when you disobey." The women and men, including Jill, screamed.

She couldn't believe how quickly her life had changed. The virus, or whatever it was, had spread so rapidly. Everyone in her household—mother, father and brother—were dead.

She had been hiding out in the house with them, keeping quiet and fighting off anyone that tried to come inside. She was lucky, she thought at the time. So many people were dying or dead, families ripped apart, literally. Jill's house had a large storage closet in the basement, filled with canned and jarred foods. But eventually supplies were needed. Her brother had gone out and gotten bitten. The idiot hadn't told anyone, but half a day later, he showed signs of the sickness, the same symptoms the news talked about, when there *was* news. His skin paled, his bones showed in places they normally didn't, and he had a high fever. Knowing he was a dead man, she and her family spent every second with him. It was the most painful thing she had ever done. She held back tears when she was with him, but always bawled when she left the room.

"We can't let him suffer like this," Jill's dad said to her and her mother. "We've seen too many people die like this. There's no coming back from it. He's almost dead . . . and then he'll come back and he won't be our Brian." Tears glistened on their cheeks as they decided. "I'll make it quick," he said, then picked up his rifle and left them in the downstairs living room.

Jill and her mother sat together, crying and shaking, waiting to hear the shot. It seemed to be taking forever, and then BOOM! They both jumped and squeezed each other tightly, their tears running together. When Jill's father didn't come down, she grew concerned. She told her mother to stay where she was and went to check on her father.

He was standing in the hallway leading to the bedrooms, holding his forearm. Jill saw the blood leaking between his fingers. His face was pale, in shock. "I couldn't do it," he said. "I just couldn't do it. Not until he turned . . ."

Jill did an about face and went back downstairs.

Later that night when her mother was sleeping, her father woke Jill. "I need you to come with me," he whispered. They went upstairs to her brother's room, his body having been removed. The bed was stained with gore where her father had blown her brother's brains out.

"I need you to kill me," he said, holding out a small revolver. "Before I turn."

She shook her head rapidly. "No, no, no." Even as she did this, she knew her father was a goner. People who were bitten didn't recover.

"I'm dead. It's just a matter of time. I'm sweating. My bones ache. I don't want to hurt you or your mother."

"I can't," she said through tears.

"You have to." Her father swayed and sat on the bed. "I don't know how much time I have left. You aren't killing me; you're saving me. I'd do it myself, but I want to go to heaven."

Jill wasn't very religious. She believed in *something*, some force that was responsible for everything, but not like her father who was brought up Catholic. He only went to church on Christmas and Easter, but held onto the things he was taught as a child. Suicide was a sin and would keep him out of Heaven. Jill felt anger building within herself. How could he ask his little girl to do this? To kill him? Would she be committing a sin? In his eyes, she might be, but in hers, she wasn't.

"Please," he begged, holding out the gun in a shaky hand.

Her insides grew cold. She went numb. The man before her was still her father, but not completely. He was half monster now, soon to become a full-fledged monster, and one that would crave her flesh. She was the last thing between saving herself and her mother. By tonight, her dad would be a member of the undead.

"Don't you want to say goodbye to Mom?" she asked.

"She won't be able to deal with it. Just tell her I love her." He paused, then looked Jill in the eyes. "I love you." He looked away. "Now do it."

Jill knew how to use a gun. Her father had shown her. Having a gun in the house, he felt his children, once they hit the age of twelve, should know firearm safety. She cocked the hammer, then pointed the gun at her Dad's head.

He glanced at her. "Not like that," he said. "You need to be closer." He reached out, grabbed her hands and placed the barrel of the gun against his temple. "Squeeze, but don't look."

Her breathing was shallow. She felt light-headed. This was it. She was going to kill her dad. No, she couldn't think of it like that. She was saving people, and ending her dad's misery. She was an angel, doing the tough work that angels did.

"I love you, Dad," she said, then squeezed the trigger. The gun roared. She closed her eyes just as her father's head jerked away. She barely heard the impact of his body hitting the mattress, then the thud of his corpse hitting the floor. She stood there, waiting. She didn't hear anything. No cry for help. No pleading. No sign that he was still alive. She opened one eye. Her dad was face down on the carpet, the side of his head where the bullet had exited was staring at her. She closed her eyes and turned away, but it was too late. She saw the pulpous, gory hole—the damaged she'd caused. She would never forget it.

She walked into the hallway, fell to her knees and wept.

"Jill!" her mother was calling. "Jill!"

Jill looked up, wiped her face. What the hell was the lady doing yelling like that? She raced down the stairs to the living room.

"What happened?" her mother asked.

"Dad was bit. He wanted me to kill him so he could get into Heaven. So I did." She had no idea why she came straight out with it. But she did. And now that it was out, she felt better. No pussy-footing about anything.

Her mother stared at her, as if she didn't understand what she had just heard. Then she said, "Oh, okay. Well, getting into Heaven *is* important."

When Manhattan was originally quarantined, Jill's mother hadn't taken the news well. They had no family or friends there, but the event itself was shocking to everyone. Some took it in stride as best they could, others flipped out. Her mother was one of the ones that didn't take it so well. She had a breakdown, hadn't been the same since. Jill almost thought it comical that the one member of her family that was the least able to handle what was going on was the one to survive.

She sat next to her mother and held her. "We need each other now more than ever. We're going to get through this. I promise."

"I know, dear. We'll be fine."

Jill was awoken that night by a gunshot. She looked around and didn't see her mother. The revolver was gone. Fearing the worst, she searched the house, ending up in her brother's room, not wanting to go there, saving it as the last place she looked. Her mother lay next to her father, a bullet hole in her head.

She spun to leave, feeling the contents of her stomach needing release, when she heard a moan. Turning back around, she saw her mother. Her eyes were open, her jaw moving slightly.

Jill's knees gave and she sank to the floor. Her mother was still alive. Jill pulled herself up and tiptoed to her mother's side. One pupil was blown; blood trickled from her ears and nose. She was trying to talk, the words unintelligible. The gun lay next to her head in a pool of blood. Jill picked it up, ignoring the warm fluid. She was angry again. Angry at the world, at her stupid father for being weak, and angry with her stupid mother for being weaker. Leaving their deaths in her hands. For a moment, just a moment, she thought about letting her mother suffer. Show her how stupid she'd been. But then Jill raised the gun and fired a shot into her mother's eye. She didn't look away. She needed to watch, to make sure she'd never do such a thing. Ending her own life wasn't an option.

After that, she packed up a few things, loaded her father's rifle, leaving the revolver in the pool of blood, and headed out into the world, hoping to find some friends, or at least people she knew.

All she found was trouble.

Men from the prison had captured her and taken her to a house up on the mountain. She'd managed to shoot one in the arm, but that was all. She was stripped of her clothing and brought before a huge, grotesque man. He called himself Cannibal. The guy eyed her up and down as he licked his thin lips. She thought she was going to be raped, but was instead given her clothes and locked in a cage in the basement along with a number of other people.

Women came and went. A few men were brought to the basement also, but kept separate from the women. She and the other prisoners were well-fed and allowed to bathe. No one knew what happened to the ones that were taken away. It was assumed they were raped and killed.

It took Jill a couple of weeks, but eventually she realized that the heavier-set females were the ones being taken away first. She was naturally thin, muscled from her years of running track and swimming. Maybe she would be one of the lucky ones.

The guards that came to check on the captives never laid a hand on them, at least not in the basement. They said things like, "He likes his women with meat on their bones," or "Cannibal will like you, sweetie." It didn't take long before Jill had an idea of what was going on. The guy's name was Cannibal. Coincidence? She thought not. The women were given lots of food, fattened up so he could eat them? No, no way. She was being ridiculous. The scumbag guards would never put up with that, or would they?

In the meantime, she kept her spirits high, looked for any chance to escape, and ate enough to stay energized.

CHAPTER 9

Cannibal sat on his throne, a chair constructed from the bones and flesh of his victims. The room had been some kind of office, having a computer desk, bookshelf and lounge chair. It was just off the living room area, the chimney there heating one of the walls in his room nicely. Cannibal made the place his, the one room where he could be himself and strike fear in the people that entered it.

He was clearly the leader. The men he had led to the mansion respected and feared him. He maintained a sense of normalcy outside of his room, wanting the men to feel safe. His way of life was not even close to what passed for normal, even among murderers, rapists and thieves. Before he'd been arrested, his victims feared him, the terror on their faces supplying him satisfaction that sex brought to most people. Here, in the mansion, the men had the same looks on their faces as his victims used to. Fear and respect worked on the inside, as well as the outside, especially in this new world. He was their leader, and though his ways were different, they would follow him. He had led them out of the chaos and into a home, a place where grand things were possible.

As long as he had his food supply, Cannibal was satisfied. He would eat *his* men if he had to, but preferred having them as soldiers. And speaking of food, his supply in the basement was running low, and with how things were these days, he didn't know how much longer he'd have the kind of fare he needed.

Before he was imprisoned, he'd had to be careful. Like all serial killers, he had to remain hidden behind a great big lie, an illusion. Create an alter ego for the public's viewing pleasure. Minding his business, never playing music too loudly, saying hello to his neighbors and washing his car on a Sunday in the driveway of his neatly, bush-trimmed home. And when he went out to fulfill his innate needs—to kill and eat—the law was ever vigilant with his kind. Cameras were everywhere. Forensics improved everyday. Remaining free and out of prison required skill and patience.

The voices, the demons, had told him he would be rewarded for his killing and eating of his fellow man. He kept on killing for years, obeying the voices until one day he was arrested, tried, and sentenced. The voices continued to speak to him, telling him to keep the faith, and that one day he would be free to consume all that he desired.

A few years after his incarceration, he heard the news, then saw it with his own eyes; the dead had come back to life. The demons told him they were his children, doing what he had already been doing. They were mindless soldiers of Hell. They would never back down or show fear and their numbers were endless. It was Cannibal's destiny to control them, but it would take time and effort on his part to complete the task. He needed to consume more flesh, and after he had been freed from prison, he saw that the voices had been correct. Now there was nothing to stop him from gaining the power of the undead, except for the undead themselves. He didn't quite understand how he was supposed to eat all that he desired if his children were devouring his cattle, but that was okay, because all was going according to plan. He'd let fate take its course.

He reached out and picked up the charred arm on the table, then brought it to his mouth and began to tear the flesh away. He hoped soon to be able to eat the flesh raw, transforming into the zombie father his children needed. Once under his control, the world would be his.

A knock came at the door.

"Enter," he said.

He knew how much his men hated reporting to him. It wasn't just that they feared him, but disliked the odor of cooked flesh and watching him eat it.

"We have confirmation that the three new arrivals have already left Cliff House," the man named Freak said.

Cannibal grinned, pieces of flesh stuck in his teeth. He had a stockpile of weapons, but the more the better. It was reported that these three had military grade weapons; weapons that would greatly help him tip the scales in his favor. The people of Cliff House would soon fall to him, this he had no doubt, then more food could be added to his pen.

"Do everything possible to take them alive," Cannibal said, pointing the severed arm at Freak. "I need more flesh."

"Yes, Cannibal," the man said, then hurried out of the room.

Cannibal tore another piece of meat from the arm. Today would be a good day, he thought. A very good day.

CHAPTER 10

Kyle Dillard turned off the walkie-talkie and removed the batteries. He placed everything in a large plastic bag, then put the bag in a metal lockbox. Secured, he returned the box to the hole in the ground. Digging even a small hole during this time of year was difficult. He'd had to use a hammer and a railroad spike to soften the earth before shoveling with the spade.

He filled in the hole, then kicked snow and leaves over it.

Kyle Dillard was a convict, sentenced to ten years in prison for driving the getaway vehicle in a bank heist. He was small in stature, thin, wore glasses and appeared as non-threatening as a bunny. He did not fair well while on the inside, often bullied and beaten, raped and robbed.

During the prison exodus—his cell door open—he remained in his cell. He hid beneath his bed for fear someone would kill him. Maybe when the prison was empty, then and only then would he attempt to leave. He figured most inmates wanted nothing more than to leave the place, not caring about settling scores or whatnot, but seeing an easy target like himself might be too much for someone who had been looking to hurt him.

When it had quieted down, hearing the occasional straggler pass by, he snuck a peek from under his bed and nearly vomited when he saw the most feared prisoner of them all, Cannibal. The monster, standing over 6'3" and weighing close to 300 pounds wasn't running like the rest of Sing Sing's inhabitants. He was standing, staring into Kyle's cell. Kyle ducked back under the bed, hoping the man hadn't seen him or would just leave him be.

"Don't be afraid, little man," the giant said. "Come on out."

Yeah, okay, Kyle thought, as urine soaked his crotch. No way in hell. Keep going you big, crazy fucker.

"I will protect you," the man said. "You shall be a member of my human flock."

Kyle didn't move and hoped the notorious serial killer would move on. Why someone would release him, Kyle did not know.

He heard the man's footsteps echoing off the floor, praying that the man was heading off somewhere else. All the other prisoners must have left by now. It was himself and Cannibal. He'd heard rumors about the big man, that he only ate hefty people. If that was true, he was safe, but it still wouldn't stop the guy from killing him. Then he thought about it; the big man had been confined for so long. It would be like locking up a sex maniac and giving the guy the ugliest girl on the planet. He'd take whatever came his way. Bony or not, Kyle was dead.

"I won't ask again," the man said. "You'll be on your own amongst your fellow inmates or food for the undead, my children."

"Children?" Kyle said aloud, not meaning to. He crouched lower and closed his eyes like a child hoping the boogeyman would go away. Time seemed to stand still. Quiet filled his ears so that he only heard the rush of blood. Unable to take it any longer, he opened his eyes and saw an oversized pair of prison-issued sneakers. He swallowed, then glanced up.

Cannibal stared back, grinning. The sleeves from his prison-supplied evergreen-colored shirt had been torn off, revealing well-muscled arms. Kyle was reminded of the time he met one of the NY Giants' linemen.

Holding out his oversized hand, blood-caked around the fingernails, Cannibal said, "It's okay, little lamb. You will be safe by my side."

Seeing he had no choice in the matter, Kyle took the man's hand and rose to his feet. He stiffened, waiting to be attacked, but the big man simply turned and walked out of the cell. "Follow me."

Wherever they went, no one bothered them. Kyle couldn't believe the carnage he saw. People were looting, shooting, stripped of body parts, eaten to the bone. The dead were everywhere. The police presence was null. It was every person for his or her self. He saw Bulldog, one of the prison's most notorious men, pummeling a woman to death just before a pack of zombies fell on him. Kyle couldn't have been more satisfied as the man screamed.

The streets were lined with vehicles. People drove over bodies—both dead and alive—and onto lawns, smashing through fences and mailboxes. But the streets were too small, the roads too clogged. Cannibal and Kyle took to the forest to make their way out of town before working their way back to the road that led to the Thruway.

They came to a house just outside of town. Cannibal smashed the door down. A family was there, the father holding a sledgehammer, the son a knife.

"Get the fuck out of my house," the man threatened. Kyle could tell he was scared and was no fighter, and if he could see that, then Cannibal did too. The big man came forward, the father swung the sledgehammer. Cannibal nimbly sidestepped the blow, then grabbed the tool with one hand and shoved the lanky man to the floor. The son came at him with the knife. Cannibal swung the tool and smashed the kid in the side of the head. A loud crunch echoed around the room. Blood exploded from the impact as the kid landed on the floor. The father howled in agony. Cannibal stood over him, raised the hammer and smashed the man's face, killing him instantly.

"What's going on, Henry?" a woman's voice called from down the hall. Then Kyle saw her, a woman in her late forties with long blonde hair and a slender build. Her eyes went wide, jaw dropped open at the carnage. She screamed, then ran back down the hall and into a room. Cannibal grinned and went after her.

Kyle remained where he was. He felt bad for the family, but if his protector needed to do *this* to others, and Kyle would remain safe, then so be it.

Screams erupted from the room the woman was in. "Mom! No!" came a high-pitched girlie scream. Kyle's heart sank a little, knowing the big man was killing two innocent women. No, one woman and a girl. He didn't want to know how old and imagined she was in her late teens. Cannibal returned to the living room holding two arms, one smaller than the other. Blood covered his chest. Kyle felt weak in the knees. Cannibal laughed. "Don't pass out on me, little man. We have work to do."

For the next couple of hours, Kyle helped Cannibal with the bodies, cutting them up and placing the parts in the oven. He threw up a few times, Cannibal chuckling at his displeasure.

When it was time for the man to eat, Kyle went into the bathroom and puked what little food he'd eaten from the household's fridge. The entire house filled with the odor of cooked bacon, which wasn't bad until he pictured what was cooking. He remained there until Cannibal called him, letting him know it was safe to come back.

"I feel good again," the man said. Grizzled bones were left on the kitchen table. Kyle guessed if he was to stay with this man, then he'd have to get used to his eating habits. Right now, the world was in chaos. He needed protection. He had no choice. If he found someone better to protect him, then he'd consider changing teams, but for now it was "TEAM CANNIBAL."

Kyle set out around the house, looking for valuables, then realized there was no place to sell them. From what he had heard, the epidemic was everywhere. What mattered now was survival gear. He found a backpack in the boy's room, antiseptic in the bathroom, a toothbrush—unopened, a bar of soap, and in the bedroom he took pairs of socks and underwear from the father's drawers, the size looking as if it would be okay. From the kitchen cabinets, he grabbed some canned goods, crackers, tea bags, and candy bars.

"We'll stay here for the night," Cannibal said. "We have a secure place and food. Tomorrow we'll head north, going over the Tappan Zee Bridge."

Kyle wanted no part of remaining in the house, but wasn't about to argue. Anything Cannibal wanted, Cannibal received. He stayed in the parents' bedroom while Cannibal slept in the living room. As long he kept the door closed, the odor of cooked meat mixed with the coppery smell of blood wasn't too strong in the bedroom.

Over the next two days, the two traveled toward the highway, staying the night in Tarrytown. Cannibal found the remains of a police officer, his Glock 21 and 3 clips still on the body. "My children don't need such things," Cannibal said, shoving the gun into his pants.

Later that same night, they broke into a home and found an elderly couple sleeping. A shotgun rested next to the bed. Cannibal slaughtered them with his knife, then handed the weapon to Kyle who waited in the kitchen with a cup of Earl Grey tea. "Now you can defend yourself."

Cannibal continued his death trek, as Kyle came to call it. The man killed many people and zombies, hating to do the latter. He rarely used the gun, preferring to use his bare hands. Kyle found more weapons along the way, a .30-30 rifle, a sawed-off twelve gauge, and a Beretta pistol.

Every night, the big man ate human meat, the whole scenario still unnerving Kyle. It was something he knew he'd never get used to. He actually thought about trying the meat, seeing how strong Cannibal was, but then realized what he was about to do and threw up.

By the time they reached the bridge, killing became second nature to Kyle.

Getting across the bridge on foot wasn't too difficult; most of the zombies were still roaming around the cities and towns. Vehicles crawled at a snail's pace. They met other convicts along the way. Only one had been a problem for Kyle when he was on the inside. Cannibal killed him one night and ate him. Kyle was grateful.

The others teamed up with Cannibal, immediately accepting his leadership. The men, killers themselves, feared the large man, even when they held guns. Kyle was in awe of his new friend and protector and couldn't have asked for anything more.

The group of fifteen men made their way up and into the mountain area. They passed many houses, mostly secluded, but finally settled into a mansion. It overlooked part of the Hudson River, had fireplaces, and plenty of room. The basement was huge and Cannibal immediately had the men go to work on making a cage.

From that point on, he ordered his flock to bring back people, people he could eat. They were not to harm anyone, and were told to bring as many females as possible—females being Cannibal's preferred meal of choice. The heftier the woman, the better.

In secrecy, the men had their fun, raping and killing, but always made sure to bring back plenty of "untouched cattle."

Over time, guns were rounded up from nearby homes. A State Troopers' barracks was broken into and assortments of weapons were acquired, including assault rifles and tear gas.

Another nearby mansion served as home to a group of survivalists. Mostly people from the community. Cannibal armed his men and sent them out to storm the place and take more prisoners, more food. But the group proved tough, not only fending off his people, but killing some in the process. He attacked a number of times, each time succeeding at only failure.

"Kyle," the big man said, having summoned the worm to his room, "I need you do something. Something very important."

"Anything," Kyle said, and meaning it, as long as it wasn't allowing himself to be eaten.

"I need you to go to them. Become one of them."

"But I—"

"You will do this," Cannibal said, softly. The large man placed a hand on Kyle's shoulder. "I told you that you would be an important part of my family. You would be needed. Do you remember this when I found you in your cell?"

Kyle nodded.

Cannibal smiled and Kyle saw pieces of flesh protruding from the man's teeth. "They will take you in. You will gain their trust. And while you're doing this, you will report back to me using one of our walkie-talkies."

Kyle didn't like this, but defying his master was not an option.

"We'll get your back-story straight," Cannibal said. "You came wandering in from another town. You said you were originally from Florida, so stick with that. You're a salesman. Remember to keep things simple."

Kyle set out two nights later, dropping the lockbox containing the walkie-talkie in the nearby woods. He dirtied himself up, ripped his clothes, then wandered down the Cliff House' driveway where he was met by armed men.

He was searched, questioned and watched closely for the first week. But he knew they would come around to trust him, or forget about him. He was an unassuming presence, a man who blended in well, disappearing into the crowd. He was small and always came off as non-threatening. He was the poster boy for judge-a-book-by-its-cover. And Cannibal must have known this, hence the reason for sending him. He couldn't let the big guy down, not after all the man had done for him.

Kyle eventually found his way alone to the lockbox, dug a hole and buried it, marking the surrounding trees so that he would be able to identify the area. He reported in a few times, telling Cannibal that all was well and not much was going on. Then, the visitors arrived with their high-powered machine guns. They weren't going to spend but a night at Cliff House. He had to alert Cannibal. He also learned of something most distressing. Not bad news for himself or the rest of humanity, but to Cannibal it would be devastating.

The undead were the result of an experiment. There was nothing supernatural about them, as Cannibal assumed. They were controlled by nanobots. A bite was not a death sentence as he had thought. Electricity of 50,000 volts or more could cure a person after being bitten. This was a revelation, and something Kyle decided to keep to himself. The information could prove costly to his life. If Cannibal found out, the man might lose it. Go nuts. The guy was on some religious crusade thinking he was going to control the things and rule the world. The men believed him too.

Kyle suddenly felt powerful.

Now, after relaying when the strangers were leaving, Kyle walked gingerly back to the house, wondering how much longer he would have to remain there.

CHAPTER 11

Jack and the others continued down the snow-covered road, the white stuff floating down dreamily. The surrounding forest was still, almost eerily so, especially when compared to the chaos of yesterday. There were no sounds of human life, from cars driving nearby, honking their horns to aircraft from above. No kids playing off in the woods—sledding down a hill, or dogs barking. Simply nothing but the muffled sound of boot hitting snow-laden pavement. But at the same time, Jack couldn't ask for anything different. He and the others would take this over the chaos any day. The land was beautiful, peaceful. He loved the city, had been there his whole life, unlike Jess who had spent time Upstate. They'd talked about moving there, and now that he thought about it, maybe they should have. Should've, would've, could've. His heart thumped hard for a moment at the thought of his wife. Damn, he missed her.

"Something up ahead," Zaun said.

Jack's pulse quickened. The group crouched, taking defensive positions. He and the others were conditioned to expect the worst.

"Road was clear when we came this way," Maria said.

They moved forward slowly, Jack watching the right, Zaun the left, Maria straight ahead.

"It's a damn body," Maria said.

Jack could only see the back of its head. The long, straggly hair draped outward, making him think it was female, but then he noticed the boots and wasn't sure. The figure's stomach rose and fell. The others stayed back a little as Jack went to check on the person.

Up close, he saw that the figure had a beard. "It's male," he said, walking around the body. The guy had a deep scar running across his right cheek and a tear tattoo below his right eye. Jack didn't like this, and immediately thought of the prisoners that had been a problem for Don and his people. But everyone nowadays had tats and he couldn't be so quick to judge.

He nudged the guy with his boot. Maybe the guy was infected, though he didn't look emaciated. He glanced back to the others and shrugged.

As Jack turned back around, he saw the man sit up, pull a snub-nosed .38 from his coat, and point it at Jack's groin. The man laughed, smugly. The crack of a gunshot sounded and the man's head exploded as the bullet tore through it. Jack looked over and saw Maria staring down the barrel of her M4.

Hooting and hollering erupted from all around. Armed men came from the woods, leaves and forest debris falling off their forms.

Jack spun around to head into the forest behind him, but more men waited there. "Don't even think about it," one said, pointing a shotgun his way. He looked over to see Zaun and Maria with their hands in the air.

The man holding the shotgun walked up to Jack and pushed the barrel against Jack's forehead. The guy glanced at the dead man, then spat on him. "I told that bastard he'd get himself killed. Not to mess with you folks."

Mess with us? Jack thought, and then he knew, this was planned. There were too many men for this to have been a "troll-under-the-bridge" scenario.

"Time to hand over the weapon," the man said to Jack. "Don't you think so?"

Jack handed over the M4, along with the other weapons he had on him.

The man grinned. "Thanks," he said, then smashed Jack in the head with the butt of his weapon, knocking him out cold.

CHAPTER 12

Jack woke up with a pounding headache. His wrists were cuffed to a steel pipe protruding from the cement wall above his head. He was seated on the floor. His shoulders ached, telling him he must've been in this position for a while.

Looking around, he saw that he was in an unfinished basement. Small rectangular windows about six feet from the floor allowed sunlight through. Zaun was to his left, chained up too. Past Zaun was a cage. It went from one side of the basement to the other. A number of women were inside it, maybe ten. Maria was with them, staring out at him.

"Good," she said, "you're awake."

"Jack," Zaun said, surprised. "Thought we might've lost you. Brain damage or something." He smiled.

"Where the hell are we?" Jack asked, his throat dry.

"They took us to a mansion not far from where we were ambushed. Brought us down here, tied us up and threw Maria in the cage. Been here since."

"How are you feeling, Jack?" Maria asked.

"Head hurts. A little woozy, but I'll live."

Zaun told Jack that they were with the former guests of Sing Sing. A man named Cannibal was in charge. The women were kept in the cages, taken one by one from time to time and never heard from again.

Jack could only imagine what these scum were doing to them. He eyed Maria and started pulling on his restraints. He couldn't let them have her.

"Don't bother, man," Zaun said. "I've tried. It's no use."

"The girls here think he eats them," Maria said, as if reading Jack's thoughts.

"What?"

"Yeah," Zaun said, "they think he's the infamous Cannibal from the news. Remember that guy? He was responsible for all those missing people in Upstate New York, Vermont, and New Hampshire. Think about it. His name's Cannibal. People are stored here, well fed, then they leave and never return."

"Wait a minute," Jack said. He thought about the name. He remembered the story. He couldn't remember which prison the guy was kept in, but it had to be him. Or maybe a wannabe. Either way, the situation just got worse.

Damn, he couldn't believe the crap they got themselves into. All they'd been through and now this. They fought their way out of Hell itself, only to become a meal for some deranged psycho? No way. They had to find a way out, and Jack knew they would. They had to. *How* was another story.

Over the next few days, Jack and the others did little more than eat, use the bathroom and bathe. One woman had been taken during that time. Sleep was virtually impossible for Jack with his hands tied above his head, but he managed as best he could. At least Maria and the women had mattresses.

A young woman by the name of Jill lost it one day, grabbing the fence and shaking it. She cried to be released; begged to know what was happening to the women.

Maria eventually quieted her down. Hours later, another girl started to flip out, only to be calmed down by Maria too. Jack understood their fear and was amazed at how strong Maria was, but not surprised.

"Damn it!" Maria shouted. "We've got to find a way out of here." She grabbed the fence and shook it with force, the jingle of the links echoing around the room.

"Forget it," one of the women said. "We've tried. They built this thing too well. And if you fight them when they come get you . . . well the last girl to do that wound up losing her head."

Zaun yanked uselessly on his cuffs, frustrated. "Damn it."

The door at the top of the stairs opened. Two men came down. One had to be close to 7 feet tall. He had long, stringy hair and a hawk-like beak for a nose. A thick metal loop pierced the flesh between his nostrils. The other man was shorter with acne scars covering most of his face. He had beady eyes, a cleanly-shaven head and stood around 5'8," but was a ball of bulging muscles.

They approached Jack.

"Boss wants to see you," the short one said. He pulled a knife from his belt, leaving the Berretta he carried holstered, and held it to Jack's throat. "Stilts here is going to uncuff you. Make a move and the boss won't need to see you anymore. Capiche?"

Jack nodded.

"Good."

The man undid the restraints. Jack's arms screamed in discomfort as they fell to his sides. He felt the blade press harder against his flesh. His hands were then cuffed behind his back, his shoulders aching from the quick change in position. Jack was taken upstairs and down a hallway, then through a living room. The place at one time had been gorgeous. Everything looked expensive. Twenty-foot high pane-glass windows took up a wall, overlooking the valley-forest below. A long sofa and loveseat took up space in the front of the gray, stone fireplace, blazing with flame. But the beer cans, alcohol bottles, cigarette butts and food wrappers decorated the vast room, turning it into a pigsty.

"Maid hasn't come yet," the man with the scars said.

The tall man left the room, returning a minute later. "Bring him."

Jack was shoved forward and back down the hallway he'd come through, winding up in a spacious kitchen.

Pots and pans hung over a center island with a grill. In the far corner was a stove. A huge, chrome-colored pot lay on a burner, the top jostling as something boiled within. A long, black and white marble counter top extended across the far wall. Two sinks rested in front of a bay window; the sink itself piled high with dishes. The ceramic tile floor was marked with boot prints, wrappers and dirt.

Jack was ushered across the kitchen, the smell of bacon in the air, making his mouth water. He exited the kitchen and entered a dining room. A white table-clothed table and ten chairs sat center. Unlit candles in silver sconces were positioned around the room. Windows, much like the ones in the living room, looked out over the forest below and the river a ways away. Sitting alone at the end of the table was a hulk of a man. He had a clean-shaven head, stubble growing along his cheeks and neck. He was holding a large piece of meat, eating it like corn-on-the-cob.

Scars manhandled Jack over to the table, pulled out a chair adjacent to the hulking man, and shoved him into it. Jack's arms were yanked upwards. Pain radiated from his shoulders to his neck. He heard the cuffs being unlocked and felt the steel leave his flesh. The huge man continued to gnaw at the meat, ignoring Jack, as if it was too delicious to notice anything else.

"Leave us," he finally said, between swallows.

The two men left the room.

Jack sat in silence, unmoving, as the man continued to eat. He didn't want to stare directly at the guy. He kept his head down, but glanced up with his eyes. What the hell kind of steak was that? It was very long and lean. The leg of some kind of animal. Then realization dawned as the piece of meat started to look familiar. His brain formulated the image. The meat ended in the shape of what looked like a hand. A human hand. Oh God. The sick fuck was eating human flesh. This *was* Cannibal.

Jack closed his eyes. He held his breath for a moment, then took a gulp of air in through his mouth, hoping to keep his gord from rising. To lose it now would be costly. He needed to be strong. This man was a monster. Opening his eyes, he waited, pretending what the man was doing didn't bother him. He knew when the monster was ready to speak, it would.

"You've come quite a distance," Cannibal finally said, placing the arm down. He picked up a cloth napkin and wiped his mouth. "Fought out of the epicenter of this apocalypse. Out of Hell itself."

Jack was completely caught off guard, and hoped his face didn't reveal it. How the hell did this *thing* know anything about him? He very much doubted either Zaun or Maria talked.

"I can only imagine what you went through," the monster continued. "What you had to endure and how many of my children you killed."

Jack felt a response on the tip of his tongue, but remained quiet. He had no idea about this man's children, but the guy was crazy, so he let him talk.

"But it is understood," the man said. "I've had to endure trials myself; including killing my own, but soon enough they shall know their father."

Jack was dealing with a real nut job. If he wasn't worried before, he was now.

"You have our weapons," Jack said, feeling the need to speak. "What more do you want from us?" The answer was obvious and one he didn't want to think about, but he had to say something.

"Yes," Cannibal said, looking at Jack. The man's eyes bore into him, sending a shiver down his spine. "Your weapons shall tip the scales in my favor. Bring me more food, and bring me closer to my destiny. My children. They are lost and without leadership or direction. They have no purpose but to eat. Once I have devoured enough flesh, I shall speak to them and they will hear me. See me as their father, their leader."

Jack found it almost impossible not to laugh, even being in the middle of a most dire situation. This oaf wasn't simply crazy, but completely wrong. Should he bother trying to explain the truth about the undead? How they are nothing more than robot-controlled corpses? Yes, he would. The whole thing might just fluster the idiot, and he'd love to see the look of utter shock and disappointment on the man's face. That's if the madman believed him. A little chaos was good in situations like the one he was in.

"I think I was brought to you for a reason," Jack said.

The man's eyebrows arched. "Really?"

"I know a secret," Jack continued. "A big secret. But I don't think you're going to like it."

The man steepled his fingers. "Please, tell me."

"It's a secret about the undead." Jack paused. Cannibal's stare bored in on him.

"It's true. My friends and I came from the heart of this epidemic. We were in an underground bunker where the 'plague' originated."

The man's face went slack. He then smiled and said, "I am on my way to—"

"You're wrong," Jack blurted, cutting off the man. "There's nothing supernatural about the undead. They're animated corpses, controlled by microscopic robots. The fucking military is behind it. The bots were designed to kill and aid our soldiers."

Jack's pulse was racing. Something inside of him snapped. He didn't care what this monster did to him. He wanted to squash the man's delusional idea on the matter.

Cannibal shot to his feet, the chair crashing to the floor. Jack tensed, waiting for the blow, and whatever else was to come. He grabbed Jack by his collar and picked him up. "I've had doubters, liars," the man said, his fetid breath assaulting Jack like a toxic cloud. "People that don't understand me or what I am." He pulled Jack close to his face. "It's scum like you that need to be removed from this planet."

Jack knew he'd gone too far. He had maybe a few moments before his life was put to an end. Maybe it was his being weaponless, or the stillness around him, or the fact that Cannibal looked like he could wrestle a Grizzly bear and win. Then again, he'd felt this way many times within the last month. But this time felt different. He imagined he'd be killed, cut up and cooked, winding up in the man's stomach, then discarded out his backside.

He couldn't go out like that. He couldn't go out at all. Not now. He needed to do something. His friends needed him. His sister needed him. This was his chance to escape, maybe his only chance. The big oaf was cocky, and had underestimated Jack when he told his henchmen to uncuff him and leave. They could be right in the other room, stirring whatever was boiling in that pot. Or they could be far away, somewhere deep in the house.

Jack brought his right knee up and into Cannibal's crotch. The big guy's grip loosened as he exhaled in pain. Jack landed another blow and was let go. He fell into his chair, leaned back, and kicked the monster in his large head as the man hunched over grabbing his groin. Blood flew from the man's lips as they split from the impact. Jack reared back both legs, the chair propped against the rear window and kicked out as hard as he could, sending the behemoth tumbling backward.

Jack leaped out of the chair, then hesitated. The big guy was down, but it wouldn't be for long. His only way out was through the kitchen. No way was he doing that. Instead, he picked up the thick, oak dining room chair, raised it over his head and tossed it at the window. The glass cracked, spider-webbing in a multitude of directions. He picked up the chair and smashed it into the glass again, his body weight behind it. The window shattered, the noise deafening. He'd have men on him in no time.

He dove through the window and onto the deck. Shards of glass sliced his hands as he landed into a roll. He was on his feet in a moment, then ran down the stairs to the backyard, and headed into the woods.

CHAPTER 13

Jack ran as fast as he could, breaking branches off trees and leaving a trail in the snow-covered ground. He winced as a maple poked him in the cheek, then carved a gash across it. Running for his life, he didn't have time to worry, or the time to dodge everything in his path. If he'd taken his time a little more, he might've been able to leave less of a trail, but all he wanted to do was get as far away from that house as possible.

He had hoped no one would pursue him. It seemed like a ridiculous notion, but it helped his mental state as he ran for his life. Then he heard hooting and hollering—and knew he couldn't slow down.

He trudged on, breathing heavy, but feeling okay. He and Jess had been runners, hitting the streets and Central Park regularly, so he didn't fear cramping up or growing tired would be an issue. The main problem would be the cold weather. He wore only a long-sleeve button down flannel shirt. The air was cold, the breaths he was taking chilling his lungs. He would sweat soon, and with sweating, came danger. Hypothermia would set in if he didn't slow down or find shelter soon, and for now he could do neither.

Gunshots rang out, but they sounded far enough behind that he didn't worry about a bullet catching him in the back. With all the trees about, it would take a close-range slug to find its way into his flesh. He guessed they were shooting for affect, trying to scare him, or maybe they were simply acting like the "cowboys" they were.

Jack kept on going full bore, sweat now lining his body. As long as he kept going, it wouldn't matter much, but when he stopped it would be an issue. For now, the adrenaline kept him going, kept him fleeing and able to fight off the chill of winter's bite.

The men continued to holler and shoot, the sounds growing louder. Bark from a nearby tree exploded. Like harmless shrapnel, pieces of it cascaded Jack's face. He ducked and decided to run in a not-so-linear fashion. It was the best he could do to avoid a bullet.

He saw a clearing ahead and burst from the tree line. He was in someone's yard. A bi-level house with cedar siding stood about one hundred feet away. A small shed sat behind the house near the adjacent tree line. Jack bolted toward the house, hoping not to feel the sting of a bullet in his back when he was out in the open.

Stairs led up to a deck, but he could reach the front of the house faster, leaving him less vulnerable to the men chasing him from the woods. Shots rang out. The air next to his left ear grew hot as a bullet whizzed by. He dove around to the front of the house and out of view of his pursuers. "He's around front," a voice called.

Jack had moments before he was either captured or killed. For a second, he breathed a sigh of relief. It felt good to be out of the sights of a gun. His mind worked sharper now. He needed to find a weapon and a defensible position, or at least put the pressure on them.

He grabbed the garage door's handle, praying it wasn't locked. The door held for a moment, then lifted, rolling up to the ceiling with a thunderous rumble. Dashing inside, he closed the door and turned the handle, locking it. A Volkswagen Jetta sat in the space. Rakes, shovels, and a leaf blower hung on the left wall. Garbage pails sat on the right. Jack grabbed one of the snow shovels from the wall and hurried up the three steps that led into the house.

The door opened to a thud. A zombie crashed to the ground. It was a woman with curly, short blonde hair and half her neck missing. Blood covered her white blouse, turning it crimson. Jack raised the shovel, bringing the sharp edge down on the thing's neck, severing it easily. He spun around and turned the lock on the door. It wouldn't keep his pursuers out if they wanted in, but it would slow them down.

Glancing around, he saw a cream-colored couch, ottoman, and a large television. Colorful artwork hung on the walls. Bookshelves lined with books took up a corner. Jack crossed the room and entered into a wide hallway. Stairs led up. He didn't know where to go and headed into the kitchen. Another zombie was heading his way. It was an older lady, missing her left cheek and hand. Dried blood decorated the tile floor. Jack dropped the shovel and grabbed a steak knife from the block of knives on the counter. He knocked the zombie's arms away, then sank the blade into the bot-controlled corpse's head and watched it crumble to the floor. Turning to the butcher's block again, he plucked another knife and wished he had thought things through. The zombies he killed should've been left for his pursuers to deal with.

He exited the kitchen and heard a crash from the living room. The men had gotten inside the garage and were attempting to smash through the living room door.

He saw stairs, but decided against going up and ran down the hall to the where the house's front door was located. It seemed pretty solid, but to each side were a row of small horizontal panes of glass. To his left and behind him, he saw another door. It was under the stairwell that led upstairs, and immediately he thought, basement.

Jack heard the splintering of wood as the living room door gave way.

The men were inside.

Screw the basement, he wanted out. He was about to open the front door when he saw a man standing outside with a shotgun. Jack dove out of the way, as a blast from the weapon shattered one of the small windows and wood frame around it.

He pushed himself up and scurried to what he hoped was a basement door and not a hall closet. Yanking the door open, his heart leaped with relief at the sight of stairs leading down into darkness. He grabbed the handrail and hurried down, but not before pulling the door closed behind him.

The gloom seemed to thicken the farther down he traveled, the light creeping in from under the door fading. Finally, he reached the bottom of the stairs to the cement floor. Looking left, he saw only darkness. Right, he saw a small window about twenty feet away, a minute amount of daylight shining through.

Hiding in a corner wasn't going to do much except get him killed, and finding a better weapon than the kitchen knife was going to be difficult in the dark. He would have to be the weapon.

He moved behind the staircase and crouched, allowing his eyesight to adjust to the environment. Gunfire came from upstairs. The men must have run into more zombies. Men shouted to each other before one said, "He went down there." Footfalls thudded overhead, stopping at the top of the stairs. Jack's heart pounded as he squeezed the knife's handle. Maybe they wouldn't come down after him. Maybe he was too much trouble.

The door at the top of the stairs opened. Bright light exploded into the basement, illuminating the staircase and immediate area below. The rest of the basement remained in darkness. Jack felt his body tensing up. He forced himself to breathe, realizing he'd have one shot at this.

"Fucking dark down there," a voice said.

"Here," another voice said.

The stairs creaked as a man descended them. Jack saw the circular shape of a flashlight's beam dance around the wall at the bottom of the stairs.

The creaking stopped. "You coming?"

"I'm waiting here in case he gets past you," said another voice.

"Come on, Scars. Grab another flashlight and come with me. Mack and Freak can watch the stairs."

"The one you got is the only one we found," came the reply.

The stairs creaked again as the man continued. He moved slowly, shining the beam on both sides of the staircase. Jack scooted underneath the structure completely and out of the light. The guy shined it on the right side, then switched to the left, almost hypnotically. Good, Jack thought. The guy was scared.

Jack followed the light wherever it shined, getting a layout of the place and hoping to catch a glimpse of an exit or a better weapon.

"I don't see nothing here," the man on the stairs said.

"Come on," said another voice. Get down there and check it out. The guy's got nothing. You see him, shoot him. If we go back without him, Cannibal's going to be pissed."

"Fucking psycho bastard."

Jack couldn't let the guy reach the floor. He waited for the stairs directly above his head to whine. Sweat dripped down his cheek, tickling him, but he ignored it, focused on listening.

The step complained.

Jack sprang out, brought the knife up behind the man's knee and sliced as hard as he could. At the same time, he saw the handgun the guy was carrying—his own .45—and reached for it. He got hold of the man's jacket arm instead, and yanked him over the railing. The gun went off. The flashlight flew from the man's hand as he crashed to the hard floor. Jack was on him in seconds, pressing the knife's bloody blade to the man's neck and slicing the soft flesh with ease. The man squirmed and clawed at his throat as Jack held him still.

Gunfire erupted from upstairs. Bullets chewed up the floor, ricocheting and pinging the surrounding walls. Jack saw the glint of metal from the .45 and dove for it, then rolled into the gloom away from the staircase.

Leaning against a wall, the darkness too much to see anything, he felt a burning pain above his left knee. He prodded the area with his fingers and winced. The clothing was torn and the area was covered in a warm liquid. One of the bullets must've grazed him. He bent the leg, put pressure on it. The pain was tolerable and would not impede him.

He had a gun. His gun. The weapon felt right in his hand. He was far from safe, but now the odds were a little better. Only a little. But he no longer was the animal on the run, unable to defend himself, having to run and hide and hope not to be found. Now, he could take different measures; fight back. Anyone that came down the stairs was getting a bullet.

Jack crept closer to the stairs, the darkness his ally.

Minutes passed. The men upstairs asked if anyone "got him."

"I think so," one voice said.

"No idea," said another.

Silence followed, then, out of the stillness, the stairs creaked again. He saw a pair of legs, then the torso. The idiot had no flashlight and was simply peering from side to side in the dark. The man held a rifle.

"Can't see shit," the man on the stairs said.

"The guy's unarmed," said a voice from above.

"How do you know that? He might have Opie's gun."

"No way. We blasted that whole area. I'm telling you, the guy's dead or bleeding out."

This was too easy, Jack thought, and took aim.

The guy kept glancing back and forth, finally stopping and staring in Jack's direction. He squinted, then his eyes went wide. Jack fired. The man's head jerked back. Grey matter exploded from the man's skull as the newly created corpse tumbled over the railing. The rifle fell to the stairs and slid down to the floor. Gunfire rang out from above, but Jack was nowhere near the bullets' area.

The shooting ceased.

"The motherfucker just killed Freak," someone said.

"He's fucking armed," another said, stating the obvious. "Going to pick us off one by one."

"Fuck this shit."

Jack eyed the rifle, wanting it, but couldn't risk trying to reach it. He was doing well. He'd taken out two men—one with only a knife, and wasn't sure how many shots he had left, so he'd have to make sure each counted.

"Where's the prisoner?" a voice asked, authoritatively.

"Damn, man," another voice said. "You scared the shit out of me."

"He's in the basement," a third voice said.

Jack could pick them off one by one, but doubted that's how this would end. He needed to do something, preferably find a way out of the basement before it was too late. Suddenly, a body came tumbling down the stairs, flopping wildly until it reached the bottom and crashed against the wall. It wasn't moving. Jack recognized the guy; it was the one from the house named Scars, his hideous markings unforgettable.

Jack swallowed, feeling the lump in his throat. He had no idea what was going on, but there was no way the man fell down the stairs. Someone had shoved him.

CHAPTER 14

Cable couldn't believe he was put on guard duty. Fucking guard duty. The prisoner named, Jack, had escaped. Cable should have been sent after him, but he'd been out scavenging when the situation occurred, returning to the house minutes after Cannibal sent men after the escapee. But guard duty? He was above this shit. As far as he was concerned, all the prisoners could die, save one. Maria.

She was like him—former military and she'd been through tough times recently. They all had, but she came from Manhattan, the heart of the epidemic. That place had been cordoned off, millions of undead everywhere. Yet she and her companions escaped, no doubt because of her training. She did *something* to him too. Stirred his loins. Her beauty and obvious warrior spirit was a complete turn on. He wanted to make her his, but Cannibal said otherwise. That sick bastard only gave the skinny bitches away—and that wasn't often.

Cable wondered why he didn't simply put a bullet into the man's head. But then he did know why, it just didn't seem fathomable.

Like the other men, Cable was afraid of the man. Maybe it was his size, the way he united the prisoners, even rival gang members, or maybe it was the fact that he ate people. It was probably a combination of all of the above. The man wasn't bullet proof, and if it came down to it, Cable could probably take him in hand-to-hand combat. Still, he didn't like being around the guy. He hadn't felt this way since he was a kid and lived with his alcoholic father. His mother had run out on them. His father turned to booze, blaming him as the reason his mother left.

"You ain't my kid," Cable's father would say after drinking a bottle of cheap whiskey or some kind of grain alcohol. "You're a constant reminder of her cheating on me. That's why she left, you little bastard. Now I'm stuck with you." Then the beatings would come, by fist, belt, or foot. Once his father held a knife to his throat, but Cable managed to get away from the man. After that night, he went to live with his Aunt. He only saw his father on occasion. Then one day the man put a gun to his head and blew his brains out.

Cannibal wasn't like that though. The man didn't drink or do drugs. He was just a psycho with a high I.Q., and for a large person, he was fast. The man had the two things needed to be a leader of the ragtag lowlifes: fear and presence. Cannibal was an alpha. As much as he wouldn't like to admit it, Cable wasn't a leader. He was an order taker. A soldier. But he was also a loner. If he had to, if the timing was right, he'd leave this place and go out on his own. For now, he had it good: a roof over his head, food, and protection. This was the whole reason he joined up with Cannibal's crew—safety in numbers. Now that things were settling down—most of humanity dead or dying, at least the local humanity, for he had no idea what the rest of the world looked like, he could figure things out. The initial craziness was over.

Cable was also a thinker. He may obey orders, but that did not mean he didn't question them in his mind. In the military, he followed orders whether those orders seemed righteous or totally fucked up. In this new regime, he had the right to disobey should he see fit. To leave should he see fit. The men under Cannibal's command were mindless, wanting nothing more than to be free, get wasted and act like animals.

Cable headed down the stairs to the basement where the prisoners were held.

"Where's Jack?" the guy named Zaun demanded. "You people are sick. Keeping us prisoner when the world around us is falling apart..."

Cable couldn't deny the statement. What Cannibal was doing to these people was sick. About as twisted as it got. But he was on the sicko's team, and these people weren't his problem.

"How can you stand by and let this happen to us?" Maria shouted.

Cable sighed. The last thing he wanted was to hear shit from anyone, let alone the cattle. Why couldn't they all just be killed and left outside where they wouldn't spoil? It wasn't like it was summer and there was a reason to keep them fresh.

"I suggest you all shut your mouths while I'm here," Cable told the room. "This is your only warning."

"Fuck you, asshole," Zaun said.

Cable felt his blood surge. For the most part, he was easy to get along with. He didn't consider himself "good" or "evil," but simply there. He acted when he felt the need, and now he was feeling it.

Cable stood in front of Zaun. He expected the man to cower, but Zaun did not. Matching stares with the prisoner, he saw a mixed bag of goods; weakness and strength, determination. It wasn't often you found both so prevalent in an individual. He'd seen it in prison, the inmates that were beaten on and raped, but had somehow managed to hold onto their pride and were never fully broken. He had also seen it in the recovering drug addict. Always a weakness present, but also the will to remain strong. This man, Zaun, was one of these people, and if he had to guess, it would be *the recovering drug addict*. This man had turned his life around, but whether it was the current state of things, or a relapse as of late, he was suffering again more than he probably had in a long time.

Cable had always been good at reading people, but prison seemed to hone this skill. Zaun was a troublemaker. Punishment was good for his kind.

Cable shot a foot forward in an attempt to kick Zaun in his head, but to his surprise, he missed. The lanky man had gotten out of the way. Then Cable found his feet knocked out from under him and he was falling. The little bastard had used his legs to bring him down.

Cable braced for the fall, then pivoted once he was down and rolled away before the prisoner had a chance to inflict real damage. Back on his feet in moments, he eyed Zaun with a grin. "Well, well," he said. "Looks like we have a—"

The door at the top of stairs opened.

"Cable," someone called. "Watch is over. Boss wants you."

Cable turned to Zaun and winked. "We'll finish this later."

He climbed the stairs, groaning to himself. He hated visiting the psycho, but at least he was getting out of guard duty.

"Track down the escapee," Cannibal said. "Make sure my men aren't fucking this up. I want Jack back here alive if possible." He glared at Cable. "I have unfinished business with him." He held up a thick finger. "But if you have no other choice, air on the side of caution, and kill him. We can't have him returning to Cliff House and warning those people."

Cable nodded. Cannibal dismissed him.

He had his sidearm, a .357 Desert Eagle. He liked power, and the weapon looked mean. Then he grabbed his Heckler and Koch G36, a sweet machine gun with a 100-round C-Mag drum magazine. Most weapons in the house, having been gathered from various residences and a State Trooper barracks, were shared. The G36 was Cable's gun. He found it a week ago in a house a little over a mile away, along with an M16 rifle, 3 AK-47's, 6 pineapple grenades, a Beretta, two 12 gauge shotguns, one a sawed-off, and a Ruger .22 pistol. The collection was an odd one. The guy must've been a collector or seller. Either way, Cable made it clear the G36 was his.

As he exited the house, he didn't think it mattered much whether the escaped prisoner warned the people at Cliff House. With the weapons found at the Trooper Barracks and the' newly acquired ones, Cannibal had enough firepower to defeat his enemy, but that wasn't the issue. The problem was the people using the weapons. Half of the men were crazed, unstable maniacs while the people at Cliff House proved to be organized.

Tracking the men proved easy. Snapped branches, trampled shrubs, and footprints made the task almost boring.

After traipsing through a densely wooded area, Cable came upon a two-story house with a moderately sized backyard. A shed sat within fifty feet of the structure. Multiple tracks led across the lawn and around to the front of the dwelling. He surveyed the scene before stepping from the woods.

The frigid wind blew, causing his eyes to tear. He heard gunfire from inside the dwelling and hurried across the open tundra, following the tracks as they led around the house to an open garage door. He shook his head in frustration at how the men had allowed the quarry to get as far as it did, especially after seeing the wide-open yard it had to cross. He stepped inside and pulled the door closed, wanting one more obstacle in the prey's path should the man make it back this way.

Cable proceeded up the steps and into the living room, hearing another set of rapidly fired shots. He gave the dead body with its severed head a quick glance, then moved past it. The men were yelling. He turned left out of the living room and down the wide hallway, sneaking up on his former prison brethren. As he stood behind them, they had no idea of his presence. He could've killed them all before they knew what was happening.

"Where's the prisoner?" he asked.

The men jumped, spinning around. Cable held out a hand and caught one of the men's rifles before it pointed at him.

"Damn, man," Scars said, "you scared the shit out of me."

"He's in the basement," Mack said.

Cable pushed past the men and peered into the darkness. A flashlight was off to the left, shining on Freak's body. Not a bad guy, Cable thought. Just stupid. Of the two men standing with Cable, Mack was all right in his book. A killer, but sane. Scars, built like a brick house and had his face cut up by his mother when he was a boy, was a sick fuck. A rapist of not only women, but of former prison mates. Cannibal never should have allowed such unstable, scum into his gang.

Seeing a sweet opportunity, Cable grabbed Scars by the neck and head-butted the guy across the nose. Blood exploded from the man's nostrils. Cable snatched the man's Glock 21 from his grip, then hurled him down the stairs. Scars tumbled head over ass, feet flying into the air only to disappear under him before he crashed to the floor and against the wall. Cable aimed the Glock at the man, ready to put a few bullets into him, but didn't. Scars wasn't moving.

Cable turned his head to Mack, who was staring slack-jawed into the basement. Mack's eyes met Cable's. "You have a problem with what just happened?"

"N . . . no way, man," Mack said. "Guy was as rotten as they come." He cleared his throat and launched a wad of phlegm down the stairs. "Far as anyone needs to know, Scars was killed by the escaped prisoner."

Cable smiled. "This 'Jack' is well-trained. Dangerous."

"That ain't no lie," Mack agreed.

"He needs to be put down," Cable added.

Mack's eyebrows bunched together. "But Cannibal said he wants him alive."

"I know what he wants, but he isn't here getting his ass handed to him, is he?"

Mack shook his head.

"We had no choice."

"No choice," Mack repeated. "Got it. I don't want to be here any longer than necessary. Fuck this prick."

"I'm glad you agree, because you were scheduled to go down next if you didn't."

The man inched back a step. "Then . . . then how are we going to kill him?"

"Wait here," Cable said. He unlocked the front door and exited the house. He didn't remember seeing what he wanted in the garage and doubted the item was kept there anyway. He went around to the back of the house and over to the shed. Removing his handgun, he blew off the lock and opened the sturdy wooden doors.

The scent hit him immediately—gasoline. There were rakes, a leaf blower, hoes, and other gardening tools on the walls. A riding lawnmower sat in the center of the small shack. In the corner on his right was the 5-gallon gas container. He picked it up, feeling its weight and guessed it was about 3/4's full.

Perfect, he thought, then returned to the house.

CHAPTER 15

Jack's mind raced with indecision. Once the stairs were on fire, he'd be trapped in the basement—unless there was a door leading to the outside. But even if there was, someone might be waiting for him there.

He bolted from the wall, ready to start shooting anyone he saw at the top of the stairs when the stairs erupted into flames. He staggered back, feeling the heat. Seeing the rifle that had been dropped earlier by the man he killed, Jack scooped it up. It was a .30-06 and in nice shape. When he escaped the basement, he'd make sure to put it to good use.

With the fire blazing, he was able to see his surroundings. To his dismay, he discovered no door, at least in the area he was in.

He shouldered the rifle and headed over to the small window he'd noticed earlier. He climbed onto the tattered workbench. The glass was too caked with grime to see through. Using his sleeve, he wiped away a small section and saw a strip of lawn and forest beyond it. He figured he was on the side of the house. Cannibal's men could be standing off to the side and out of view, but he had no other choice but to escape via the window.

Simple turn-style latches at the bottom of the window kept it locked. He saw hinges at the top and realized it opened outward. He turned the latches and tried the window, but it wouldn't budge. He pushed harder, but still nothing. Breaking the glass was an option, but he'd prefer to avoid making that much noise. He pulled the .45 out and began hammering its butt against the lower part of the window as smoke choked him.

Eyes watering, he banged harder, and finally the window gave. He tossed the rifle out first, then crawled through. He was up in an instant, .30-06 in hand, and realized he was indeed at the side of the house. Without wasting another second, he sprinted into the woods.

Jack worked his way about ten feet in, then went right to circle around to the back of the property. He crept up behind a thick Maple and saw two men standing on the far side of the backyard. What they were doing there—he did not know.

He backpedaled quietly and traveled left until he had a view of the person-less front yard. If he had to guess, he'd say Cannibal had sent four or five men after him. Two were now dead, which meant only two or three left.

Jack made his way to the backyard again and saw the two men standing there. They were easy targets, talking, guns pointed at the ground as if they had nothing to worry about. Jack aimed the .30-06, but held his fire. If the sights were off, he'd miss at this range. He needed to make sure his first shot was a kill shot. He retreated into the woods again and worked his way around to their side. The closer he came to his targets, the slower he moved, avoiding branches and leaves. The snow wasn't thick and made a soft crunching sound. At about thirty feet from the targets, he smelled cigarette smoke.

"Damn," one of the men said. "Motherfucker is burning."

"Guy's dead for sure," said the other man.

Jack decided not to try and get any closer. From his position, he could see one of the men clearly. Raising the rifle, aiming, he pulled the trigger. The gun jumped, the retort loud. He saw his target jerk forward as blood and gore exploded from the head. The corpse hit the ground as Jack stepped from behind the tree, ready to end the second man's life—but there was no one there.

Gunfire erupted from Jack's left. Bark from the tree next to him splintered into pieces like exploding confetti. He dove to the ground and scurried behind a tree.

Damn it, he thought. He really screwed up. He should have kept an eye on both men. No time for second-guessing now. The gunfire stopped. He peered around the tree, staying low and saw no one.

His attacker was hiding, most likely waiting for him to pop out, then BAM!

Jack crouched behind the tree, the trunk wide enough to shield him. He took deep breaths, calming and readying himself for what ever was to come. The silence was deafening, almost screaming at him.

Jack's best bet was to move. He was in a forest. Bullets traveled straight. The trees would serve as natural shields. He stood a good chance of avoiding getting shot as long as he had a good head start. He got to his feet, took some deep breaths, then bolted from the oak.

Gunfire erupted from behind. He felt a sharp sting in his right shoulder blade and cried out, stumbled a little, but was able to continue running. He moved around and between close-together growing trees, just like he did earlier when he was running from Cannibal's house. Bullets pinged from all around him. Branches broke and the snow burst at his feet. Whoever his pursuer was, he was good with a gun.

Jack's shoulder continued to scream with pain. He wondered how badly he was injured. Adrenaline might be the only thing keeping him up, and when that wore off, he would go into shock.

Fighting through the pain and fear, he kept on, his breaths coming harder and harder. Every so often, gunshots rang out from close behind, making him flinch, the hurt in his back worsening as if someone were pressing a hot iron to it.

Maybe it was best if he stopped and returned fire. It wasn't like he was unarmed. Jack saw a thick tree trunk up ahead and ducked behind it. He heard his pursuer's footfalls and fired blindly from around the tree, hoping to slow his attacker and make the guy take cover, giving him a chance to recuperate.

Bullets riddled the tree that Jack was behind.

Now that he'd stopped running, he felt the weariness of "fight or flight" creep in. He was tired, winded. His shoulder and leg hurt, but he still felt good enough to keep going. Stopping had been a bad idea. He fired a couple of rounds in the direction of his attacker, then took off running. He'd dig in and fight when he had no other choice, but while the adrenaline was still pumping, he'd used it.

Not more than a minute later, his body began to tire again, his energy seeming to dissipate rapidly. The pain in his back and leg was worsening. His pant leg was covered in red. Just when he thought it might be time to stand and fight, he saw a clearing up ahead. Sunshine made the snow-covered field shine in an almost blinding fashion. He couldn't enter the open area. He'd be dead in seconds. It was time to stand and do battle. Then he saw them. Five figures walking toward him. Friend or foe, he did not know. If they were the latter, whether he entered the clearing or not, he was a dead man—boxed in. Friend, and he had a chance.

Jack ran from the forest. "Help!" he yelled, though it came out horse and low.

He fell to his knees, tripped up by something, a snow-covered branch or rock. This was it one way or another. Killed or saved.

"Jack?" a voice called out. "Is that you?"

Focusing, Jack recognized the person. It was Paul from Cliff House. Duane, Mark, Rob and someone he didn't recognize were with him. They all held rifles.

They hurried forward.

Jack waved his arms. "Wait," he said, trying to warn them.

Cable stood just inside the tree line, his form hidden behind a tree. He aimed at Jack. This was too easy. He almost felt like closing his eyes, at least to make the shot somewhat difficult.

Jack had been a worthy opponent. Proved to be more than just a civilian. The type of quarry that deserved a better death. Instead, Cable aimed his G36 at one of the men in the field. They were also easy targets, but he didn't know them. Didn't share the hunt with them.

With the squeeze of his forefinger, he fired the gun and watched the man he had in his sights go down. A dead center kill shot. The others returned fire in a panic, the shots random and none threatening. Cable waited until the gunfire stopped, then retreated. He would deal with Jack at another time, should fate warrant it.

CHAPTER 16

Jack and the others made their way back to Cliff House. The man who had been shot was dead. His name was Mark Jones. Jack couldn't help feeling it was his own fault, and wondered why the man that had chased him hadn't shot him instead.

On the way to the house, his shoulder barking and bloody, Jack told the tale of how he, Zaun, and Maria were ambushed and taken to a house not far from where they currently were.

"We were kept in a basement; Zaun and I were chained to a pipe. Ten others, mostly women, were locked in a cage. I was brought to a man named Cannibal."

"We know of him," Paul said in disgust.

"The sadistic monster was eating a human leg," Jack said. "I think all those people in the basement are food. We have to get them out of there."

"First we need to get you to Cliff House and to the doc," Duane said. "We'll talk about what we're going to do when you're fixed up."

The group rested a few times, taking turns carrying Mark's body. Jack wanted to help, but was too injured and needed his strength. Makeshift bandages were applied, but it did little to stop the bleeding in his back.

At the house, Jack's wounds were tended to by Darcy Kloom, a nurse who used to work at a nearby hospital. Cliff House's garage had been divided into an infirmary and surgical center. Darcy was not a surgeon, but between herself and Jim Gunner, a veterinarian, they did their best when someone was injured. Fortunately for Jack, Jim wasn't going to be needed today.

"You're lucky," Darcy said, "bullets must not like you."

Jack truly had been lucky. The graze on his knee was just a burner, the skin sizzled away. His back proved worse, but not as bad as it could have been.

"No way was this a direct shot," Darcy said as she examined him. "I'd say you caught a ricochet. The bullet's lodged against your scapula, but there doesn't appear to be much damage." Jack was given a rolled up cloth to bite down on as Darcy plucked the slug with a pair of forceps. Both wounds, along with some scrapes, were disinfected and bandaged. With no working hospitals around, and very little in the way of on-hand antibiotics, infection was something a person did not want to deal with.

Jack thanked Darcy, who told him he should rest.

"I'd love to, Doc, but there's too much at stake."

He headed upstairs to Don's room, desperately needing to talk to the man.

The bedroom was a fair size, probably the master suite. Windows on one side of the room were completely boarded over while windows that looked over the valley were not. A queen-sized canopy bed took up much of the floor space to the right, along with a rich mahogany bureau and makeup piece including a chair and long mirror. In the corner was a matching-in-style upright dresser, the doors closed.

On the other side of the room, sitting in front of a working fireplace, was a plush, purple ornate-looking sofa and a dark, cherry-colored, leather recliner. Don was adjacent to these items, sitting at an executive's desk and writing in a notebook. He looked over. "Jack," he said jovially, then rose to his feet and hurried over to him. "Looks like Darcy patched you up pretty well."

"Yeah. She did a fine job."

"I'm so glad you're okay. Come, let's talk." Don walked over to the fireplace and sat on the recliner, keeping it upright.

Jack took a seat on the sofa, wincing as he did so.

"Darcy give you pain meds?"

"I didn't want any. Save them for people who really need them."

A low burning fire danced in the hearth, the warmth welcoming.

"I'm sorry about Mark," Jack said.

"Yes," Don said, nodding. "Me too. He was a good man. A hard worker and well-liked."

"Did he have family here?"

"No. He came to us after his wife was killed."

Jack shook his head. "Again, I'm terribly sorry."

"Anyway," Don went on, "I heard about what happened to you and your friends. I must apologize, Jack. I thought we'd scared those people off."

"You couldn't have known."

"Would you like a drink of water?" Don asked.

"Sure."

He got up, grabbed a bottle of water and handed it to Jack before sitting back down.

Jack unscrewed the top and drank about half the water before replacing the cap and setting the bottle next to him.

"They have our weapons," Jack said, looking Don in the eyes. "It'll help them if they plan on attacking you again. We're talking flashbang grenades and machine guns."

"It is definitely a concern, but what I'm more worried about are your friends and the others you say are being held there."

"We have to rescue them." Jack said. "The sooner the better. And we need to discuss Cliff House's situation."

"Situation?"

"Those men out on the road were waiting for us. They knew we were coming."

Don's eyebrows shot up. "How can that be?" Then, as quickly as they went up, they furrowed. "Wait . . . what are you saying?"

"You have a mole in Cliff House."

Don let out a breath, looking dejected.

"There is the possibility that we were followed from the bridge when you rescued us, and Cannibal's men simply waited for us to leave."

"No," Don insisted. "No way. We made sure the area was clear before we left for the bridge and no one was following us on the way back."

"Then you've got a traitor amongst you."

"Imposs—" Don began, then stopped himself. He shook his head slowly. "It just can't be. Everyone here is . . . like family."

"You know them all, personally? From before everything happened?"

"Most, but not all."

Jack inhaled, feeling a stab of pain in his upper back. "Now that I'm here, whoever the mole is will want to report back. You need to keep an eye on your people. And keep this conversation, this knowledge, between only the few you know you can trust."

"Right." Don nodded, seeming to stare off into space.

"Step up patrols. Get the lockdown established. No one in or out. Only put guards on ground duty who you *know*. And be ready—because they're coming. Cannibal is one sick man, and now that he's armed, he'll be even more dangerous. It's only a small number of guns added to his arsenal, but it could mean the difference."

"Thanks to you they're down three men. That should aid in our favor."

Don went into action with Jack's help. Security patrols were stepped up. The house was locked down. Members were going to pull extra duties, gathering food and supplies. People looked scared and tired. During dinner that evening, Jack saw defeat in their eyes, something he didn't see the first time he'd walked into Cliff House.

"Don," Jack said, later that evening in his room. "I'm really worried about the people here. They don't look so good."

Don smiled and put a hand on Jack's shoulder. "We'll be okay. These folks have been through a lot. They're resilient. And they can all handle a gun."

Except for Don, Duane, and Paul and a few others, the people of Cliff House didn't seem like they were ready to go into a defensive war, let alone try to save Maria, Zaun and the others. Cannibal's people were vicious killers, and wouldn't hesitate when it came time to do what must be done. Don's people had fought off those same men, but now the stakes were upped.

"And I know we haven't found the spy yet, but I don't think we can afford to wait around to see who it is, or for Cannibal's attack."

"What are you saying?"

"That we attack them first." Jack watched as Don's brows knitted together. He imagined having to work the man hard, convince him that going on the offensive was the right idea, but the man appeared to be thinking.

Don nodded as he rubbed his chin. "That's an interesting idea."

Zaun, Maria, and the rest of the people being held at Cannibal's might already be dead. Don had the numbers and most of the people were capable of using a firearm, but that didn't mean they were marksmen or soldiers, cut out for infiltrating a heavily armed enemy. Defending a home from intruders was one thing, going out and acting like a soldier was another. Suddenly, Jack's idea wasn't looking so great. But he couldn't let his friends die over there. He had to try and save them. If he had to, he'd go alone.

"We've always been of the defensive mindset," Don finally said. He paced back and forth. "Fortify, and defend against any danger. With Cannibal having extra weapons, and a spy, if there is one, staying put here might not be the best thing for us."

"It won't be easy, but if we defeat Cannibal, we'll get rid of a growing threat and save a lot of people. By attacking first, we'll catch them off guard. They'd never expect it."

"I like it," Don said, "but we have to find the traitor. This won't work if the mole relays our plans. Without the element of surprise, we won't stand half the chance."

"I agree."

"But even before that, I need to talk to the others here about the plan. Convince them. I may be the "leader" so to speak, but I cannot order anyone to do anything."

"I understand."

"Any ideas on how we are supposed to find the spy?"

Jack smiled. "Call a meeting. Announce the plans to attack. Then keep an eye on who leaves the house. We'll flush the bastard out."

"It's risky, but I don't see any other choice."

"It's the best option."

That night, a meeting was called. Everyone not on duty gathered in the living room, the people on patrol already filled in on the goings on. Don spoke about the plan to attack. The mood in the room seemed to darken as hushed whispers broke out. People were afraid, wanted to leave. Find another place.

"We cannot run," Don proclaimed, standing on a chair next to the fireplace. "They could attack at any time. If they catch us as we're leaving, we'll be slaughtered, or worse, taken prisoner and eaten by that devil. If we strike first, and hard, we can defeat them and free those poor souls trapped there. In this time of peril and mayhem, there needs to be a voice of right. I know it's scary, but I feel this is our best bet."

Jack sat back and watched the people's faces. They were quietly chatting among themselves. Duane and Paul had been informed of the plan before they headed out to patrol and were already onboard.

"You don't know me," Jack said, standing, "but I've come a long way and been through much, like many of you. I've seen bad men, and this Cannibal is one of them. He's thriving in this new world. We can't let this happen. He'll only get stronger over time. He's overconfident, and now is the perfect time to strike. Citizens just like you are being held prisoner over there, kept in a cage waiting to be slaughtered and eaten. This has to stop. Those people need to be freed."

"We can do this," Paul said, entering the room, having finished his patrol duty. "The ones who guard the house, like me, all agree with the plan and what must be done."

An elderly man stood up. "I'm with you all."

Soon the room was aloud with talk and the consensus was in. People were still clearly frightened, but the resolve to fight was present.

Don clapped his hands. "We get ready tomorrow. Plans have been drawn up for those of you that won't be coming with us and for the children. A day from today, we'll march on that evil place and show those men that their kind aren't welcome around here."

The next day the house bustled with activity. Supplies were gathered, including food and essentials. Jack, his shoulder still aching, sat in the living room and loaded bullets into magazines. The group had a nice assortment of rifles, handguns and shotguns, but no automatic weapons or explosives, at least not until Paul came in to show him what he'd been up to since last night.

"We found a bunch of these about a week ago." Paul was holding what used to be a small propane tank, the kind used for backyard barbecuing. All around the white canister were nails and screws—stuck to the thing with some kind of resin. What appeared to be a fuse was leading up to the spout. "Turn on the gas, light the fuse and run like hell."

"Roll them in like barrels or plant them somewhere when the enemy is attacking?"

Paul grinned, pleased with himself. "You got it."

"Great job. I'm sure they'll come in handy."

Jack was pleased to see the ingenuity being used. Don had said his people were resilient. Jack hadn't seen them in action, and wondered how tough they were, but so far, he liked what he was witnessing.

CHAPTER 17

Kyle sat on his bed in Cliff House, nervously twiddling his thumbs. He had dire information. The people of Cliff House were planning an attack on Cannibal. The big guy, his boss—the man that had saved him, wouldn't expect such an act. Wouldn't be ready for it. Kyle had to warn the man before it was too late.

The original reason he was sent to Cliff House was to spy, reveal the place's weak points, guard rotations, best times to attack and if possible, sabotage weapons, the food supply or whatever. Now that Cannibal had greater weapons, including those taken from Jack and his friends, maybe it didn't matter if Kyle's *real* home was attacked. No, he couldn't think like that. He needed to get word out, and quickly.

Grabbing his jacket, he went over to the bedroom window. Maybe he should stay where he was. Join Cliff House and get rid of the others. No. He'd never amount to anything here. With Cannibal, he was someone and was counted on for important work. Plus, he owed Cannibal. That man might be sick, but that man also saved him, made him an integral part of his operation. Kyle was playing a significant role, maybe the most vital.

Under Don, he was a garbage man, collecting the trash, disposing and burning it. He cleaned the bathrooms and outhouses. Don had said he'd find other jobs for him, but since he was the last to arrive and the work needed to be done, it was Kyle's responsibility. Kyle was an educated man. He had a degree in science and was planning on going to MIT before his "episode."

Screw Don and the people of Cliff House. No-good, snobby-nosed assholes, he thought. Looking down upon him, belittling him with such menial tasks.

Kyle pushed the curtain aside and glanced out the window at the lower roof. He'd used the window as an exit before, traveling across the angled surface to the ladder that was attached to the house, then down it and into the forest where he radioed Cannibal or whoever was listening. During daylight hours, he had simply said he was going for a walk around the property and wouldn't travel more than twenty feet from the house. Once inside the woods, he'd dart into the forest and make his way to the walkie-talkie.

Kyle reached up and undid the latch at the top of the window, then pushed up on the frame. The window squeaked as if in pain. He froze, then continued opening it so that he had just enough room to escape. With the lockdown in place, he had to be extra careful. If he was caught, he'd just say he was going stir crazy and needed to get out—and they would believe him, because Kyle was just that kind of a guy.

CHAPTER 18

Duane tugged the wool hat over his ears again, the thing rising over time, and made sure the zipper on his jacket was all the way to the top. The frigid wind gusted against him, finding his exposed flesh like some invisible entity. That was better, he thought as his ears were shielded again. He was on guard duty, patrolling from the roof. Paul was on the other end behind one of the chimneys. Normally, their jobs were to watch over the surrounding areas, but today they had added responsibilities. Anyone caught coming or going was to be reported, stopped if possible. Getting off the roof wasn't too difficult; ladders had been nailed to the sides of the house at certain locations shortly after Cliff House was established. It made it easy for the guards to get around and for people to escape in the event of a fire. With all the open flames, lamps and kerosene heaters, fire was of a huge concern.

On top of the added duties, Duane was told to keep an eye on Kyle, since he was going to be on watch-duty directly over the guy's room.

"Why, Kyle?" he had asked.

"He was the last one to arrive here," Don told him. "I'm not saying he's done anything wrong, but being that no one here knows him, I think it's best we keep a close watch on him. On everyone, but specifically him."

Duane found it almost laughable that the man could be a spy until he thought about it. The little guy was unassuming and blended in. Physically, he wasn't a threat. So maybe he did make for the perfect spy.

News of Jack's capture and escape, along with what was going on over at Cannibal's house was unnerving. He hated waiting here. Jack was correct. They needed to get ready and storm that wicked place.

As he looked out over the property and surrounding woodlands, a noise from below caught his attention—a window in need of lubrication.

His pulse quickened.

He crept over to the edge of the roof and peered down at the roof below. To his right was Paul and Greg's room. On the left was Kyle's, which was more like a converted closet. It had been used for storage until the little man arrived.

From his vantage point, Duane couldn't see which window had opened. If he leaned out any farther, he might fall. So, he waited.

He thought about getting Paul's attention, but the man was on the other side of the roof. He didn't want to miss a chance at seeing the person leave the house. There was a chance someone was just opening a window for some fresh, winter air, or a smoke, but he doubted it. With the house as cold as it was, fresh air was far from needed. If someone had opened the window to have smoke, he saw no flicker of flame nor smelled the pungent odor of tobacco burning. Duane couldn't remember if Greg or Kyle were smokers.

He saw movement from the room on the left, Kyle's window. A jolt of angry heat coursed along his spine. He bit down, feeling the urge to pounce on the person, the traitor. Maybe it was nothing. An innocent act. Duane needed to see this out before he did anything.

A leg extended from the window, the foot touching down onto the roof. Then the torso and head.

Hot damn. It was Kyle. That little bastard. They'd all welcomed him, taken him in, given him food and a place to stay. Duane fought against yelling out, wanting to let the little fucker know he was caught, but the smart thing to do was to follow the man. See where he was going, and maybe who he was meeting.

Duane scooted back, not wanting to be seen should Kyle look up. He heard the window close, waited a few seconds, then peered over the edge and saw Kyle, hunched over, creeping along the roof to where a ladder had been attached to the side of the house.

As soon as the little bastard was out of view, Duane rushed to the nearest ladder and hurried down to the lower roof. He knocked on Paul's and Greg's window, hoping Greg was there. He couldn't see inside due to the window being blacked out—most of the smaller windows, the ones that weren't shielded by plywood, had removable boards against them. It was decided that the enemy didn't need easy targets; especially at night when someone's silhouette might show against a light source, like a flashlight or even a kerosene heater. All of the larger windows along the side and front of the house were boarded over with plywood, held in place by screws and nails.

As moments ticked by, Duane grew impatient. Kyle was getting away. He couldn't risk losing him. Then he saw the hue of the window change, the plywood board having been removed on the inside. Greg eyed him for a second, then opened the window.

"What's up?" he asked.

"Need you to alert Don, then get Paul. He's on the upper roof. Kyle just left through his window. I'm going after him."

Greg nodded and left.

Duane ran across the roof. At the edge, he glanced down and took in the yard. No sign of Kyle, but there were tracks leading from the ladder. Duane scrambled down, hit the ground with a thump, and took off toward the woods, rifle in hand.

Once inside the tree line, he slowed, listening. He heard nothing but the howl of the wind and proceeded onward, following the tracks. He walked for about five minutes before he heard a rustling noise from ahead. With so many trees, both leafless and pine in his path, he couldn't see what it was. He moved forward slowly, stepping in the same set of tracks he'd been following, hoping to lessen the sound of crunching snow.

A shot rang out, and Duane felt a whoosh of air against his cheek. Another shot quickly followed and the part of the tree next to him exploded in a spray of bark. He ducked behind the nearest tree, a thick oak. The shots were coming from where the tracks led.

Damn it. The little bastard had spotted him.

Duane crouched, picked up a small branch and tossed it out. Two more gunshots sounded. So the little guy was jumpy. Good.

By now, Paul knew what was up. The gunshots would've alerted others as well. They'd have Kyle eventually, dead or alive.

Duane couldn't wait for the cavalry. Kyle could still get away. He needed to keep the guy here. He removed his hat and poked it out from the left side of the tree. More gunshots rang out, but they weren't very close. He peered from the right side of the tree while wiggling his hat on the other. Kyle was about twenty feet ahead, crouched low behind two close-together trees. Duane pulled his hat back, took aim with the rifle and fired two shots, both wide on purpose. "The next one is for you," he shouted.

Kyle fired three shots in response, none of them aimed.

"Why the heck are you shooting at me in the first place?" Duane asked, hoping to throw the guy off.

Two more shots were fired, the bullets spitting up snow and forest debris a few feet to his right. Duane wondered why the man was shooting so erratically, not bothering to aim his shots, or run away. Taking a chance, he peered out from behind the tree.

Kyle was reaching down, not even looking in Duane's direction. He pulled something from a hole. A pile of dirt was next to him. The object was rectangular and black. Duane had a clear shot if he wanted one. Kyle held a black stick in his other hand, then attached it to the rectangular object. Duane's eyebrows rose. The little bastard wasn't rendezvousing with someone or leaving messages under a rock; he was using a walkie-talkie.

One thought flashed across Duane's mind; he needed to stop Kyle from alerting whoever was on the other end of the line. He took aim and fired.

CHAPTER 19

Jack was resting in the living room, halfway to Sleepville when he was startled awake. It was Don, and he looked like he'd run a mile. He was breathing heavily, excited. "I think we found our mole," he said. "Duane was on duty when Kyle left his room through his window. Shots were just heard to the east."

Jack got to his feet, his back biting.

Don motioned for him to stay put. "We have it covered. Duane and some others have gone after him."

"I've been sitting here doing busywork. It's time I made myself useful."

Don nodded. "If I can't convince you to rest, then come on."

Jack threw on his coat, grabbed one of the rifles off the table, the .45 already in his holster, and hurried outside. He ignored the pain as best he could; knowing much more was at stake. He entered the woods, following a multitude of tracks that were all leading in the same direction. Don remained behind with a few others, taking up watch just in case this whole thing was some kind of diversion.

A few minutes of trudging through the forest, Jack came upon the others. Duane, Paul and Greg were standing around Kyle's corpse, his lifeless eyes staring up at the treetops. Blood reddened the snow around his body.

"Shit," Jack sighed.

"Yeah," Duane said. "Had no choice. He was using this." Duane handed Jack a walkie-talkie.

"Guess we definitely found our rat," Paul said.

"Did he radio anyone?" Jack asked.

"Not sure. He was holding it to his face . . . It's why I shot him."

Jack pounded his fist against a small pine, knocking a flurry of snow free.

Silence followed for a moment. Then a rustling was heard in the distance, catching everyone's attention. The forest was moving, getting closer, as if it was alive. Jack's eyes widened. Not alive. Undead.

"Fuck me..." Duane uttered. "All that shooting must've alerted a horde in the area."

"Back to the house, now!" Jack ordered.

The group took off for the house. Jack wasn't worried about anyone getting in trouble. The distance to the house wasn't too far, but once they were there . . . well that was another story. This was the worst time for a zombie assault. Ammo, resources and energy would now be used, and they needed those things for when they attacked Cannibal.

The group made it to the house, Jack and the others yelling, warning the people who were out on the deck. They had only minutes to spare. Arms were taken up by most. People gathered along the deck's railing and from windows and the roof.

The undead shuffled from the tree line. Ten became twenty. Twenty became forty. Shots were fired, the air filled with man-made thunder. Jack was afraid the noise might attract more undead, but with so many already here; there was no choice in the matter.

From the deck, he took out as many as he could, trying not to waste a shot. But with so many coming, it was difficult. The mass reached the house, slamming into it like a tidal wave. Arms reached up, fingers grasping for him and the others. Jack saw heads explode. Body parts fall from torsos. The air was rank with death and cordite, an odor in which he was all too familiar.

A young boy named Derek was positioned next to Jack. The kid couldn't have been older than ten. He was holding a Ruger .22 and blasting away. His shots weren't rushed. The kid wasn't overly excited from what Jack could tell. His eyes were focused. He was on a mission. Maybe later, the event would unsettle the lad, but for now he was acting like he'd been born to do this.

Jack heard a scream. He looked up and saw a body fall from the roof. It landed in the horde and was quickly swallowed as undead began to tear away at its flesh. The screams lasted a few seconds.

Jack couldn't tell who it was. He looked at the kid next to him. Derek was wide-eyed and slack-jawed. He'd stopped shooting. And just like that things had changed for the kid, becoming too real. Jack wondered if Derek knew the person.

Jack grabbed the kid by the shoulders and turned him his way. "It sucks, but keep firing. We need to do him justice and slaughter these things. Keep everyone else safe."

The kid nodded. Still seeming in shock, he took up shooting again, but the vigor from his eyes was gone.

When the last shot was fired, about sixty dead lay in the yard. Guts, brains and scattered pieces of rotting flesh lay about. The clean up would be horrible, Jack knew, but the bodies couldn't be left to rot. He feared the bridge had been compromised and this was only the first wave, but that proved not to be the case, as no more undead arrived.

He was tired, achy, but rest wasn't an option. The bodies were gathered and burned, which took a couple of hours, then he and the others went back to work on preparing for the assault.

CHAPTER 20

When Cable finally returned to the house, he went straight to Cannibal. The big guy was furious. "I expected more from you, Cable," the man said, then tore the fleshy piece of rib bone from the torso that was on his plate and tossed it across the room in anger. Cable took the verbal assault that followed, knowing if it came to blows, he could hold his own, even against such a foe. Cannibal had hardly ever laid a hand on his men—he never had to—but he did threaten to do so, by raising a hand or standing face to face, mere inches apart. They all feared him and did as he asked, even the craziest ones. With Cable, this never happened. Cannibal kept his distance. Maybe the big guy never laid a hand on Cable because he knew the man was dangerous and didn't want to test the waters. At least that's what Cable wanted to believe, plus he was far more valuable alive than dead.

"Get everyone together and make sure those fools are ready," Cannibal ordered after his tirade was over. "Weapons checked, magazines loaded. We're attacking in two days. We can't afford to lose any more men, or all the weapons we've acquired won't mean a thing. Cliff House has valuable supplies and food, food we can both benefit from."

After leaving Cannibal's repulsive quarters, Cable went room to room alerting everyone to the boss' orders, then went to his own room for some alone time. He felt hollow. Unfulfilled. That man, Jack, had eluded him. When Cable set his sights on a person, that was it, the individual never got away. Angered, he smashed a fist into the sheetrock wall, creating a large hole. For sure, Jack was with Cliff House now. After Cannibal's assault, many would be dead. Jack included. As far as Cable was concerned, Jack was his to finish, but there was no way he could put a "do not kill" order out on the man and expect it to be obeyed, especially with the group he was going into battle with.

Come to think of it, Jack's friends were anything but normal people. They had been through Hell. Survived against tremendous odds, odds Cable wasn't sure he could've endured. Alone, Jack had killed all the men sent after him, and the guy had started out without a weapon. Cable needed something to fill in the void he was feeling. If he couldn't have Jack, then why not Jack's friends? Zaun had proved dangerous earlier, and he did have a score to settle with the man.

Things were on the brink. Change was about to happen, whether Cannibal won this small battle he was preparing for or not. Many people were going to die. Would the prisoners be left to sit in the cage in the basement while the full-on-assault happened? Or would Cannibal worry and kill them all. No, not all, just the dangerous ones, like Zaun and Maria. Those two didn't deserve to go out like that. They were warriors who deserved a fitting end. A chance. True, they were prisoners, but not of any war. Just of some maniac who liked to eat people.

Enough was enough. Cable had had his fill of this crazy place and its killers, rapists and common scum. He wasn't like them. He was above them. It was time to move on, but first he had a minor score to settle in the basement. Win or lose, it was the proper thing to do.

CHAPTER 21

Pain and stiffness radiated down Zaun's arms and into his shoulders and back. His neck was cramped too. No matter how much he tried to move, eventually the position he was in—sitting on the floor, hands tied above his head—got to him. The only time he was allowed to lower them was when it was time to eat or use the bathroom. Two guards would stand before him with guns trained while he did his business. The task was humiliating. He was at least thankful that the people in the cage turned away as he did his business.

Since Jack's escape, a guard had been stationed outside the basement door. The individual checked in on the group every so often. Zaun wondered why a guard wasn't stationed *in* the basement. Why at the top of the stairs? The only thing he could think of was that Cannibal didn't want the temptation of the women to cause one of his scumbags to act inappropriately with his food.

Sitting there, trying to adjust his position to a more comfortable one, Zaun heard the door open at the top of stairs.

"Hey, asshole," he said, "I need to use the bathroom."

"Piss in your pants for all I care," the reply came.

He heard a conversation. Two men were talking. Then a large, well-built fellow came down the stairs. Zaun had seen him before. His name was Cable.

"Cable," the guard said, hurrying after the burly man. "I don't think you should be here. Cannibal said no one is allowed in the basement."

When Cable reached the bottom of the stairs, he spun around, grabbed the guard by the head and twisted it to the left. Zaun heard a popping sound as the vertebrae clacked together. The man went instantly limp. Cable let him drop to the stairs and crumble to the floor.

Zaun's heart was in his throat. He had no idea what was happening. Maybe this guy had had a change of heart and was going to free them all, but something inside him said otherwise.

Cable rifled through the man's pockets and pulled something out. He held up a small key. Eying Zaun, he said, "I think we have a score to settle," then walked over to him. He placed the key in Zaun's hand and stepped back. "Free yourself." He then removed his coat and tossed his sidearm across the floor where it rested against the dead guard.

Zaun hurried to undo the cuffs. His arms fell to his lap. Painful relief burst from his shoulders.

Arms wide, Cable said, "I am unarmed, except for that which I carry inside me. I'll give you a minute or two to stretch out your muscles."

Zaun couldn't believe it. The psycho was releasing and challenging him to a fight. It wasn't just his muscles that needed a moment, but his mind too. This was too surreal, but it also might be the only chance he and the others had to escape. Cable was clearly doing this on his own, and there was no telling when someone might come along. He needed to kill this man quickly and get the girls out.

"End me, and you'll have a chance at freedom." Cable pointed to the dead man. "You'll have two weapons, mine and the guard's. And I'll even throw in a bonus. Upstairs is a locked room. Inside is a stockpile of weapons. Guns mostly. Newly acquired since the last time Cannibal attacked Cliff House. Weapons from a State Trooper's barracks, along with a private citizen's highly illegal collection. Cliff House won't stand a chance. Get past me, flee the house, and you can warn your people."

Zaun didn't know whether to believe him or not, but figured the guy was telling the truth. He had no reason to lie. He looked toward the cage and caught Maria's glare. "Kill him," she said.

Zaun rolled his shoulders, rotated his arms, kicked out his legs and loosened his neck. He also cleared his mind as best he could.

The pressure on him was insurmountable. If he failed, everyone died.

"Ready?" Cable asked, bending his knees, arms out. His hands weren't balled into tight fists. They were loose, ready to be squeezed on impact, Zaun knew. The man was much larger than he was, but as Zaun learned long ago, size didn't always matter.

His pulse raced as he prepared to fight to the death; at least he imagined it being to the death. Cable hadn't exactly said what would happen, but Zaun assumed the winner wouldn't ever be getting up again.

Zaun stepped forward, keeping his stance low. Cable stepped forward as well. The two men circled each other, neither taking their eyes off the other.

"Kill him, Zaun," Maria said. The other girls were quiet.

Zaun shot forward, then jigged to his right and launched a fist high. Cable sidestepped a fraction of an inch and Zaun missed. Committed to the move, he could only follow through and was met with a knee to his abdomen. He went with it, collapsing his center and absorbing the blow as best he could, letting the air out of his lungs and caving-in on himself. At the same time, he let his arms fly toward his attacker's face, fingers pointed outward. Zaun felt them make contact, then heard the guy grunt.

Backing away, catching his breath, Zaun saw Cable rapidly blinking his left eye. But the guy remained in a fighting stance, facing Zaun, preventing him from attacking with ease. Cable winced as the two men continued to circle each other.

Zaun faked a kick on Cable's left side, then switched to a punch, but his opponent was ready for it. Cable bent low, then lunged forward and slammed his shoulder into Zaun's ribs.

Zaun had just enough time to brace himself, extending his legs back to keep from falling over. Instead, the man hammered Zaun into the wall. Pain exploded in his back as the breath was knocked out of him again.

Fighting through the pain, Zaun brought his elbow down on Cable's spine, again and again in furious fashion and felt the man's hold loosen.

Cable slid down, wrapped his arms around Zaun's legs, and pulled him off his feet and into a sitting position. Zaun slapped the man's ears as hard as he could while drawing in a much needed breath. Cable sat up quickly, flung Zaun's arms out and started reigning down blow after blow to Zaun's face. Zaun covered up, deflected a few punches, but the ones that got threw were sledgehammer-like. With each hit, Zaun saw stars. He knew he couldn't remain where he was for much longer and survive.

Using his arms, Zaun wrapped up Cable's arms. He wouldn't be able to keep the man locked up for long. He pulled himself up and smashed his forehead into the man's nose. He felt it crunch, then saw blood explode from both nostrils. He released his grip on Cable's right arm, then reached up, curled his fingers around his attacker's ear and yanked.

Cable howled as his head jerked sideways. Zaun took advantage and ripped part of the ear free, the tearing of flesh and cartilage almost sickening. Cable jerked back. Zaun brought his right leg up and shoved Cable off, having just enough room to push himself to his feet. Cable was hurt, but far from finished. Blood gushing from his head, Cable grabbed onto Zaun's right ankle and yanked him to the ground. As he went down, he sent a chopping-hand into Cable's throat, then rolled to the side.

Zaun was back on his feet in seconds, the big man clutching at his throat, coughing. Zaun launched kick after kick into the man's side and felt a few ribs give. This fight was to the death; rules need not apply.

Cable spun on him, reaching for anything, but Zaun jumped back and out of the man's grasp. Cable tried getting to his feet, but Zaun came in and hit him square in the face with a kick. Blood flew as the man arched over. Zaun jumped onto the man's back. Cable, weakened but not done, bucked wildly, forcing Zaun off.

Cable was on one knee, rubbing his jaw and grinning. He spit blood, then said, "You're one tough little dude, but if all's you're going to do is tick tack me to death, then we're going to have to up the game." He reached behind and pulled out a small, three-inch blade knife that was curved like an eagle's talon. He launched himself at Zaun. Zaun stepped in and parried Cable's knife-arm, then sent an open-hand strike to Cable's chest, followed by a knee to his groin and an upper cut to the face, sending Cable sprawling backward.

Zaun glanced around the immediate area looking for a weapon, but saw only the cuffs. Cable's gun was across the room.

The man was already rising to his feet, grimacing, but ready to continue the fight. Zaun rushed in with a kick, but Cable caught the leg and sunk the three-inch curved blade into his calf.

Zaun cried out. Cable had opened a large gash. Blood soaked his pants and dotted the concrete floor. Zaun kneed Cable in the side of his head, then backpedaled away, leaving a trail of red behind.

Cable attempted to rise, but fell over. He clutched at his chest, wincing. The earlier palm strike had done its job, internally damaging the big man—to what degree Zaun didn't know.

"What the fuck," Cable said, spitting up blood. He tried getting up again, but couldn't.

"I wouldn't move if I were you," Zaun said.

The fight was over. Zaun hurried as best he could to where Cable's gun lay and scooped it up. He racked the slide on the .357 Desert Eagle, then fished out the sidearm, a .45 Berretta, from the dead guard's holster.

Holding the .357 out, he walked over to Cable.

"Kill me quickly," Cable grunted. "Don't let me die slowly like this." Zaun bent down, smiled, then whacked the guy across his head with the butt of the gun, sending Cable into unconsciousness.

"Get the keys," Maria said. "They're on the guard."

Zaun limped back to the corpse and retrieved a key ring, then returned to the cage and unlocked it. The prisoners filed out one at a time, most whimpering with relief.

Maria told everyone to be quiet. "We're not nearly out of the woods yet."

Zaun handed her the Beretta. She popped out the magazine. "Feels full," she said, then slapped it back in place and racked the slide. Smiling, she patted Zaun on the shoulder. "You did great."

One of the girls started kicking Cable in the ribs. "You sick piece of shit," she said. Maria ran over and wrapped her up in a bear hug. The girl's name was Jill. She was from the area and had lost her entire family, starting with her brother. Out of all the women, Jill seemed the most unflappable, yet the angriest.

"He deserves to die," Jill said, "like the rest of these scum."

"Yes, he does," Maria said, "but we need to worry about leaving here. Get your head on right and pay attention. Can you do that for me?" The girl's face screwed into a scowl of hate, but nodded her compliance.

Zaun called Maria over. "Should we leave him?"

"I don't like it, but yeah. Leave him. Doesn't look like he'll be much of a threat anyway."

"Depending on the damage," Zaun said, "he might not make it."

Maria grabbed the cuffs that had been used to lock Zaun up and cuffed Cable's hands to his feet. "That should help."

A woman named Margaret picked up Cable's coat and put it on. "Sorry guys, but I'm freezing." No one seemed to care.

Maria tore some fabric from Cable's shirt and wrapped it tightly around Zaun's still-very-much-bleeding leg. "You're going to need something better, but for now that's about the best I can do."

"Thanks," Zaun said.

"Okay, everyone," Maria said, "it's time to leave this place."

CHAPTER 22

Maria led the group up the stairs, Zaun at her heels. She cracked the door open, listened, then poked her head out. A hallway extended a short distance in both directions. She looked back at Zaun, motioning for him and the others to follow.

She had no idea which way to go and thought about heading upstairs to the weapons room, but didn't want to risk it. Cable might've been lying, but even if he hadn't been, the room might be locked. And, even if they got their hands on some more weapons . . . would the girls know how to use them properly? They'd most likely get mowed down in a firefight. It was better to get out of the house as quickly as possible. She decided to head left down the hall.

She came to a closed door, listened for a moment, then moved on, coming to an open door. She peered around the frame and saw that the room was void of life, but filled with plenty of death. Along with a long leather sofa, a wall-mounted television, and an enormous oak desk with an executive chair, were the heads of various animals—three deer; a moose; an alligator, and a lion. Maria wondered how long it would be before human heads lined the walls. She closed the door and moved on.

The hallway opened up to a spacious living room accented in light browns, the cream-colored carpet now sodden with dirt and grime. Maria stepped forward, telling the group to stay back. A three-piece couch, loveseat and ottoman took up space around a grand fireplace. Maria could feel its warmth from across the room. A large television was attached to the brick above. The far wall on her left was composed of what had to be twenty-foot high windows with a view of the snow-covered valley below. An oversized ceiling fan hung from the rafters. A balcony looked over the room, accessible from the second floor.

Voices came from a doorway in the far right hand corner of the room. Maria hurried back to the group in the hall. "Go, go," she whispered, and they scrambled into a state-of-the-art kitchen that could've been the feature of a cooking show—had the ceramic tiled floor been cleaned, but was now laden with boot prints, stains and trash. A slender, bald-headed man with a long scraggly beard stared at Maria, then eyed the group. "What the—" he began, dropping his can of beer to the floor. He reached for his rifle, an M4 that had been resting against the counter.

Zaun pulled out the knife he took off of Cable and threw it at the man, hitting the guy square in the head. The blade didn't connect. The knife bounced off and hit the floor. The man grunted in pain and stumbled into the wall. Zaun scooped up the weapon and tackled the man, sinking the blade into his Adam's apple, preventing a call for help. Blood spewed as he pulled the weapon free. The dying man clutched at his throat, gasping for breath that would never come. Zaun grabbed the guy's head and twisted, breaking his neck.

Maria had the M4 in her hands. "Get his jacket off," she said, "it's cold out and we may need it."

Zaun removed the coat. Blood soaked part of the right side where the zipper ran. He went through the pockets and found a set of keys, a magazine for the M4, a pocketknife and two pieces of chocolate. He handed the coat to Maria who handed it to Jill, telling her to put it on.

"I'm not wearing this," Jill said. "It's got that scumbag's blood on it." She passed it to Margaret who already had a coat. Margaret passed it to Georgina who passed it to Susan who dropped it to the floor as if it was diseased. Maria couldn't blame them for not wanting to wear it, but this was about survival.

Zaun tossed the chocolates away. Maria looked at him. "I'm not eating anything that came from that man's pockets," he said.

Maria grabbed the bloody coat from the floor and put it on. If no one else was going to wear it, then she would. Compared to what she'd had to endure overseas, wearing a coat with a little blood on it was no big deal.

"Let's move," she said.

They headed into the dining room and Maria's heart leaped in her chest at what she saw. Along the right wall were more huge windows with an incredible view of the mountainside, but it was the blue tarp taped in place, fluttering noisily as the wind crashed against it, that made her smile. A way out.

She approached one of the windows and peered out. She saw no one, but that didn't mean sentries weren't about. She and the others couldn't remain in the house much longer. In fact, she could hardly believe their fortune so far.

"We're leaving," she said. Ripping down the tarp wasn't an option and Zaun's newly acquired pocket knife wasn't sharp enough. Any guards passing by on the grounds would clearly notice the missing material. She went into the kitchen, opened a few drawers until she found one with knives and grabbed a sharp one before returning to the tarp where she cut a slit down the middle. She poked her head out. Her eyes teared as frigid winds blew across her face. She made sure the area was clear, then stepped out onto the deck that ran along the back of the house. From here, she had a better view of the backyard.

Zaun poked his head out. "We good?"

"For now, so move it."

The others came from the slit, Maria and Zaun keeping an eye out. When everyone was on the deck, Maria led the group to the stairs and proceeded down.

When they hit the yard, Maria feared being seen. They were out in the open with nowhere to hide. Anyone looking out one of the windows would see them. Only a shout or gunshot would let her know if their escape was going to remain smooth or not.

There was quite a difference in the way Cliff House was operated when compared to Cannibal's. Cliff House was well-guarded and fortified. There was no way they'd have escaped the place, at least without being seen. Don had guards everywhere, patrolling the grounds and the roof. Cannibal's henchmen seemed, for the most part, to be lazy and not very bright, save one or two of them.

Maria couldn't help but wonder if an attack on Cannibal was a good idea. Why hadn't Don considered it? It was worth a few casualties to be rid of the scumbag and his minions. Then again, Don and his people didn't know how Cannibal ran the ship— careless and lax. A surprise attack would be perfect. Sure, Cannibal had the weapons to take out a small army, but not an organized one that used the element of surprise. These criminals were overconfident and more of the "attack" frame of mind. Don and the people of Cliff House were more of the "defend" mentality. Maybe with Maria's information, she could help plan an assault that would end Cannibal's rule. If Don waited for an attack, she feared the worst for Cliff House. Defending against so many guns, even ones used by such idiots, could prove detrimental.

At the bottom of the stairs, the group huddled close together.

"I'm going to run across to the woods first," Maria said. "When I think it's safe, I'll wave you girls over. Then Zaun."

"Why not all at once?" Margaret asked.

"I'm going to be able to cover you from the tree line. Zaun's going to stay here and act as additional cover should we need it."

"It's okay girls," he said. "Maria knows what she's doing."

Maria bolted across the open yard and into the forest. There, she hid behind a wide tree, rifle at the ready, and peered up at the house. All seeming quiet, she motioned for the girls.

Jill led the way as the females ran, hair flying wildly, arms waving at their sides.

A rustling noise from behind drew Maria's attention. She quickly scanned the woods behind her. Seeing nothing unusual, she put her sights back to the house. As soon as the girls reached her, she told them to take cover, then motioned for Zaun.

Eyeing the house, she saw movement at the blue tarp. The barrel of a gun poked through the slit.

She couldn't warn Zaun fast enough as the gun fired.

Zaun went down.

Electricity coursed through Maria's veins. She took aim at the tarp and fired three shots. She heard a yelp as the gun barrel disappeared back inside.

Zaun lay face down in the middle of the yard. She needed to get him out of there. The whole place would be crawling with Cannibal's men. She called Jill to her, the only one of the girl's that wasn't curled up into a ball.

"We've only got seconds before this place is under full assault." Maria pulled out the .357. "You ever shoot a gun before?"

"Yeah, my father's .45, but only for fun."

"That'll have to do. Remember the kick?—well this one's going to have a bit more. I'm going to get Zaun. You see anyone, start shooting. Don't worry about hitting anyone, from this range you won't. It's just cover fire, keeping whoever is up there wary of showing themselves or getting an accurate shot.

Jill looked hesitant.

"You can do this. Just point and shoot. Keep a firm grip."

Maria slung the M4 over her shoulder, then bolted from the tree line and reached Zaun in seconds. He wasn't moving. The left side of his face was covered in red, the snow beneath it too. She didn't have time to examine him, and hoped she wasn't going to be carrying a corpse. Thankfully, Zaun wasn't a big guy.

Maria grabbed Zaun from behind by his armpits and began backpedaling toward the forest, keeping an eye on the house. She was an easy target for a halfway decent shooter. A window on the second floor opened and the barrel of a rifle extended from it. Shots were fired. Bullets kicked up the snow to her left. From behind, the .357 sounded and tufts of wood siding exploded about ten feet from the gunman's position. Jill's shots were nowhere close to the shooter, but seemed to do the trick as he ducked back inside.

Almost at the tree line, she heard one of the girls scream. She reached the forest and pulled Zaun in about ten feet before dropping him to check on the girls.

"Jill," she called.

"Over here."

About fifteen feet in, a body lay on the ground. It smelled of death and rot. Its clothes were torn and ragged. Clearly a zombie. Then Maria remembered hearing the rustling noise.

"Fucking undead came out of nowhere and attacked Susan," Jill said.

Susan was on the ground, eyes wide in disbelief. Her hand was bleeding.

"Where's Margaret and Georgina?" Maria asked.

"They took off after the zombie bit Susan."

"Bit?"

"Yeah."

"Damn it," Maria hissed.

"What about her?" Jill said, pointing the .357 at Susan.

"Lower the weapon, Jill," Maria said.

"But she's infected," Jill insisted. "She's as good as dead."

"We can save her."

"No. No you—"

"Jill. Trust me. We can save her. I have to check on Zaun. Lower the weapon and keep an eye out. We'll be all right, okay?" Maria turned away and headed to Zaun. She knelt next to him and found a pulse. Relief flooded through her.

Voices came from the direction of the house. Shouting, then shots were fired. Bullets whizzed through the forest and pinged off trees. The shots were clearly random. Thanks to the number of evergreens along the tree line, there was no way anyone could spot their position, but they'd have to move.

Maria lightly swatted Zaun's cheeks. "Wake up. Wake up."

He stirred, eyes opening. "What's going on?"

"Hold still while I take a look at you," she told him. A dark, almost black line ran along the side of Zaun's head. "You've got a burner. You'll live."

"Hurts like hell."

"Can you walk—" she began, but was silenced when gunfire sounded from the woods. The girls!

She helped Zaun up, put his gun in his hand and told him to follow her to where the others were. When she reached Jill, her mouth dropped open. On the ground, her brains strewn like a dropped melon, was Susan.

"What. Did. You. Do?"

"I wasn't going to let her suffer," Jill said, coldly. "You were wrong to lie to her."

Maria felt her insides boil. Her finger twitched against the trigger of the M4. Red flashed across her vision and she wanted nothing more than to kill this girl. This scared, stupid girl.

"You idiot," she scolded, and tore the gun from Jill's grasp, then brought her arm back, ready to strike the girl.

"Go ahead," Jill said, not flinching, "I'm not sorry for what I did."

"You will be," Zaun said. "We could've saved her. We know how. We've saved many before her. Myself included."

More shots rang out. Bullets cut through the trees, some nearer than others. Everyone crouched.

"We need to leave," Zaun said.

"No," Jill said, looking stricken. "She was a dead woman. There's no coming back."

"We spent a lot of time together in that cage. I told you about the bots and how they work," Maria said. "I reiterated here and you still didn't listen. You're a murderer."

"I don't believe you," Jill said, her face rigid.

"Why would we lie?" Maria asked.

"We. Need. To. Move. Now," Zaun insisted. "We'll sort this out later."

"She's not coming with us," Maria said.

"Yes she is, and she's the one that has to live with it."

Zaun might be partly correct, but Maria was already blaming herself. She saw the look in Jill's eyes. She never should've left her alone with Susan.

"You guys are serious?" Jill said, incredulously. "You're wrong; there's no cure. The dead are damned."

Maria grunted, shook her head in disgust, then headed deeper into the forest, following Margaret's and Susan's tracks. She couldn't believe she'd sat there arguing with the girl when bullets were flying, a girl was missing, and their escape was happening.

As they made their way through the woods, the sound of gunfire lessened, but the tracks now had blood around them. Someone was hurt. The amount of red in the snow grew more apparent the farther the group traveled. Something bad must've happened. Someone was hurt.

They picked up the pace. Maria's feet were freezing now, soaked from the snow going over the tops of her boots, but she trudged on, knowing stopping would do nothing. The others were just as cold and tired. There was more blood, as if the wound was gushing. Then she saw it, about ten feet away. Georgina was kneeling by Margaret's prone form.

"Shit," Zaun said, from behind.

Maria hurried to the women. Margaret's body was completely surrounded by red snow. She knelt next to the woman and felt for a pulse. Nothing. "She's gone." She looked up at Georgina, tears streaming down her cheeks.

"There was nothing I could do," Georgina said. "She never said anything. I looked back and saw her face-down in the snow."

"What happened?" Zaun asked.

"She probably caught a bullet," Maria said. "Those maniacs were shooting wildly."

A small, ragged hole could be seen in the girl's jacket just above where the right kidney was located. Slipping her hands under the body, Maria flipped it over. Margaret's dead eyes stared upwards. Her entire shirt was soaked in blood. Pieces of slushy red snow stuck to her. A large, gaping hole took up her abdomen.

"She's dead," Jill said. "We need to keep moving."

Maria stood, faced Jill. The girl for the first time appeared nervous. It took all she had for Maria not to lay Jill out. She turned back toward Margaret and began kicking snow over the body. Zaun helped.

"I knew her for only a short time," Georgina said, "but she was a good person."

"I know," Maria said. "We'll miss her, but we need to move."

The group trudged on, following Maria. No one said much. Georgina was still in shock, but managing. Zaun took up the rear, Jill in front of him.

"Do you know where we're going?" Zaun asked.

"Nope," Maria said. "Hoping to hit a road soon."

The others, even Jill, put their trust in her, because no one said another word. A short time later, they came to a road. One way led up the mountain, the other down. They went up.

They came to an intersection. Maria thought it looked like the one she'd seen while riding in the armored truck, then again she wasn't sure. Everything looked similar—trees and more trees and snow. Lots of snow. They turned left and followed the road, grateful to be out of the forest. Unfortunately, the road was covered in at least a foot of snow. Maria no longer felt her feet, hands or face. Zaun was shivering. Jill seemed okay, oddly enough. That bitch was colder than the air.

Ten minutes later, they came to the somewhat-shoveled driveway that led to Cliff House. Zaun laughed in relief.

"We made it," he said.

"Put your weapons away unless you want to get mistaken for the enemy," Maria said.

She and the others marched down the driveway, guns tucked away or slung over shoulders.

Halfway to the house, three armed men came from the woods and surrounded them.

CHAPTER 23

Cable awoke. His head pounded, but it was his chest that really ached, feeling as if an anvil had been dropped on it. But the pain was inconsequential. He was more concerned about his predicament. He had no idea how long he'd been unconscious, but he had to leave as soon as possible. When Cannibal found out he was the cause for the prisoners' escape, he'd be a dead man. Every man in the house would be after him. He had no friends and most of the other men would gladly like to see him gone.

Footsteps clomping on wood shook Cable from his inner thoughts. His pulse quickened. He scooted around to get a better view of the stairs and saw that it was former inmate, Billy Bob. Billy Bob wasn't the man's real name, but he was a hick if there ever was one, with missing front teeth, unwashed, messy hair, a scraggly, unkempt beard, and a belly that rivaled a pregnant woman's.

"What the—?" the man scoffed.

"Get over here and uncuff me."

The oaf hurried the rest of the way, stopping when he hit the ground. "Where's the prisoners?"

"Get me out of these chains, you moron."

"Holy shit, they escaped! I got to tell Cannibal."

"Release me first," Cable hissed. "They just left. I can hunt them down while you tell the boss. You wouldn't want him asking why you left me here when I could've been after them, would you?"

"No . . ." The dumbass appeared to be thinking.

"Stop standing there and un-fucking-cuff me," Cable demanded, snapping Billy Bob into action. The burly hillbilly kneeled by the dead guard and fished around in the corpse's pockets until he found the handcuff keys, then hurried over to Cable and undid the man's wrists and ankles.

Cable shot to his feet.

"I'll tell Cannibal," Billy Bob said. "Hell, I'll alert everyone." The redneck turned to leave. Cable grabbed the man by his wild mane with one hand, slid Billy Bob's knife from its place at his hip with his other, then yanked the head back. With the man's neck fully exposed, Cable ran the blade across it with as much force as he could muster. The flesh parted; the cut deep. Blood spurted across the room. Cable released the hillbilly who fell forward, clutching at his throat. The man turned over, staring at Cable with disbelieving eyes before the light went out of them and he fell limp.

Cable dropped the knife on the man's belly and headed up the stairs.

He opened the door and saw that the hallway was clear.

He went to the second floor where his room was located and grabbed his pack—already filled with a few days supply of non-perishables, soap, a toothbrush, extra ammo, flint, matches, and a change of socks and underwear. He'd learned in both the military and in prison to always be ready to move.

His Heckler and Koch G36 assault rifle was also kept in his room, secured in a locked case, of which only he knew the combination. He also had a Kimber Tactical .45 handgun stashed in the wall behind a poster. He'd gotten the weapon off a dead detective. He had seen the body lying in a ditch, the badge gleaming proudly off the pig's belt. The weapon fired smoothly and felt perfect in his hand. But more than that, it was a reminder that the law no longer applied to him or anyone else.

He opened the box and strapped on the .45's gunbelt, then shouldered the HK G36 assault rifle. Anyone seeing him leave might be suspicious of him, but no one save Cannibal would dare ask him what or where he was going.

He went downstairs and out the front door. Mack was standing guard.

"Cable," he said, "what's up, man?"

"You didn't see me," Cable responded, staring the man in the eyes.

"Uh, okay. Whatever you say."

"You're all right, Mack. It'd do you good to get away from here. This place is just like prison, but without the walls and cells. Same people, same mentality."

He turned and headed toward the woods. Cable had remained with Cannibal longer than he thought he would have. The episode in the basement was the final straw, and he guessed it was a definite way, win or lose, to get his ass moving. Cannibal was a crazy, sick bastard. A man like that would eventually fall one way or another and he didn't want to be around when it happened.

CHAPTER 24

Jack lay in bed, sleep eluding him. Tomorrow was a big day. He and the others would be going into battle. They would have the element of surprise, which should account for a swing in Cliff House's favor, but they would be using semi-automatic, lever-action, and bolt-action rifles, along with handguns, shotguns and homemade bombs against whatever Cannibal had in addition to the M4's, frag grenades and any other weapons the maniac had acquired. Unlike the people of Cliff House, who had dug in and rarely went out for supplies anymore, Jack assumed Cannibal had people scouring the area.

The M4s and frags shouldn't make that much of a difference. It would come down to sheer will, numbers and fire power. Who had more . . . Jack didn't know for sure, but most of the people from Cliff House seemed like they could be counted on.

He also worried about Zaun and Maria. What would happen to them during the attack? He had no idea if they were even alive. Maybe his escape had triggered Cannibal to act, to kill his friends as immediate payback.

A knock sounded at his door. "Jack, it's Paul."

Jack jumped out bed, his shoulder reminding him that he was still healing. He unlocked the door and opened it. Having lived in the city his whole life, and having been through hell itself he still felt the need to lock his door—even in the confines of Cliff House.

"What's wrong?"

"Zaun and Maria are back."

Jack just stood there, confused. Were they back in pieces? Sent in a box?

"Jack?" Paul said, smiling. "Your friends are alive. Zaun's getting patched up down in medical along with a young woman; Maria's in the living room."

Jack followed Paul to the first floor before Paul headed off for patrol. The living room was crowded with people. Everyone turned when Jack entered the room. The crowd parted almost magically. He saw Maria, along with a young girl that Jack remembered from his time in Cannibal's basement. Her name was Jill. Don was standing across from them. Maria's face lit up, matching Jack's expression. He walked over and wrapped Maria up in a big hug.

"It's so damn good to see you," he said. "Both of you."

When they parted, Jack saw a teary-eyed Maria. She blinked rapidly, preventing any liquid from reaching her cheeks. Jack let his tears fall before wiping at them.

"How is Zaun?" he asked.

"He'll be okay. A little banged up. If it wasn't for him I don't think we'd be here."

Maria went on to explain everything, from Zaun's incredible fight to their escape into the woods. There was a lull in the conversation just after the group entered the woods. Maria's story stopped flowing, as if she were omitting something, or trying to remember it, or possibly making something up. Jack could be wrong, but he knew her well enough to know something was up.

"And the four of you are the only ones to survive?" Jack asked.

Maria nodded. "It was almost too easy though. I mean they didn't pursue us."

"It *wasn't* easy," Jill said, "but we did what we had to do."

Maria glanced at Jill with a look of extreme contempt on her face, but only for a moment, then it was gone. Something must've happened between them. Jack had seen that same expression back in the city after Zaun's apartment-hunting excursion that brought a crap-load of undead down upon them.

"Well," Don said, "it doesn't appear that you were followed. So count your blessings." Don looked at Jill. "And what's your name?"

"Jill. Jill Hannigan."

"Good to meet you, Jill," Don said, holding out a hand. She took it and they shook.

"So, the house is only full of Cannibal's men?" Don asked. "All the prisoners are free?"

"I think so. At least in the basement. The cages are empty now," Maria said.

"How about some payback?" Jack asked.

"Payback?"

"Not sure if you're up for it, but we could use another gun," Jack said. "We're launching an attack on Cannibal. Take out him and his men once and for all."

Maria shook her head. "I don't think that's a good idea."

"Why not?"

"They've got weapons. Lots of weapons. Besides what they took from us, they raided a State Trooper's barracks. They also found some automatic weapons at a house. Cannibal doesn't sit around. He's always looking for more firepower and food."

Jack sat stunned. He looked at Don.

"You think they'll be on alert now?" Don asked.

"This sure does change things," Jack said.

"We can't attack," Don said. "And now we're sitting ducks."

Talk burst out amongst the crowd. Worry and panic spread.

"People," Don said, ushering everyone to quiet down. "This isn't good news, but we can't panic now. We have to remain vigilant and focused. Just like we have been."

"We need to leave," someone said.

"Pack up and go," said someone else. "Find another place far from here and start over."

"Don," Jack said, "running won't work. You'll never get far enough."

"I don't know if we can stay here, Jack. If what Maria said is true, and they let her and the others escape, it was only because they are planning to attack us soon. I don't see any other option."

Jack had an idea. He'd thought about it last night, but it was crazy—especially while Maria and the others were still being held prisoner. With them free and this new information, Jack's idea might be their only hope. Sure, it was nuts, but it was something— and it was better than running. Cannibal's grasp would only grow if he took Cliff House for himself. There was no way these people could pack up everything quickly enough and take it with them. They'd leave behind too much, and like prey that runs from a lion, the lion will chase, capture and eventually kill it.

"I have an idea," Jack said. "You all might think I'm crazy, but I think it's worth a shot."

"Let's hear it," Don said.

"Have your people start packing immediately. Thin out what they may have already packed. They'll need to be able to move quickly."

"Okay, people," Don said. "Pack up essentials in the event we need to move out tomorrow, then get some rest, as difficult as that might be to do."

As much as he wanted to check on Zaun, Jack went upstairs to Don's room with Maria. He wished Paul and Duane in on this, but they were still patrolling.

"Are you nuts?" Don asked, after Jack presented his idea.

"Wait," Maria said, "I think it might just be the best bet."

Don paced, rubbing his stubbly chin. "I think we should just leave. Take what we can, and go."

"Where?" Jack asked. "How far do you think you'll make it? You've got a few elderly and children. And you'll have Cannibal on your trail. Do you think he won't be able to find you? If you had a week's head start, maybe, but a day?"

Don's face was drained of color. The man looked truly worried. Digging in and staying put proved much easier, especially when fighting off the enemy had worked repeatedly. Now he had a tough decision to make, a different mindset to take.

"I need to talk to the others," he said.

"Don," Maria said, putting a hand on his shoulder, "I know this is a tough thing to consider, but I really believe it's the best option considering everything."

Don said nothing, only nodded.

"I know it's a lot to think about," Jack said. "We'll leave you to it." He and Maria headed for the hallway, Jack stopping in the doorway. "If my plan works, you'll never have to worry about Cannibal or his people again. And you'll have access to all those weapons." With that, he closed the door.

Jack and Maria went to check on Zaun. He was lying on a cot. A kerosene heater sat a few feet away, keeping him warm. He had a bandage around his head and leg where he'd been stabbed.

"Doc said I'd be okay, just need rest," Zaun said.

"That's great news," Jack said. "I heard you're quite the hero."

"Nah," Zaun said. "Maria would've figured a way out eventually."

Maria smiled at that, but shook her head. "I know you didn't have a choice in the matter, but you fought well and smart. I was impressed."

"Awww, you're making me blush," Zaun said, grinning.

Jack told him about his crazy plan, and how Don was thinking it over.

"Damn," Zaun said. "That is nuts, but I agree with you guys. I don't see a better solution to Cliff House's problem."

"Well," Jack said, "we don't want to keep you up. You need your rest."

"Good night, Zaun," Maria said, then kissed him on his forehead.

Neither Jack nor Maria received much sleep that night. Early in the morning, Don came and woke them, telling him Jack's plan was a go. The people had packed up as much as they could carry and fit into the vehicles.

After getting dressed, Jack, Maria, Zaun, Duane and Paul got together in Duane's room and worked out a plan. The house would be vacant soon, with two groups of residents heading in different directions to safe houses chosen in the event of an emergency. Each house was about a mile away. If Cannibal's men attacked before Jack's plan got off, at least the people would be split up. Maybe only half would be hunted down while the others managed to get far enough away. According to Don, there were other survivors shacked up in various places—they simply didn't want to shack up at Cliff House, preferring to go at it with their own groups, or head somewhere else. Sure enough, many of those became Cannibal fodder.

When he thought about it, Jack imagined there were hundreds, maybe thousands, of people scattered all over, surviving. Not everyone could be dead or undead. He wondered how many. It seemed like Cliff House and Cannibal's house consisted of the last survivors on the planet, but Jack knew this couldn't be the case. And it made him feel better. Like any other creatures trying to survive a terrible situation—and during the winter—people wouldn't be out and about. They'd be hunkered down and hidden.

With Zaun's injuries, he would have to sit this adventure out. And as much as the guy protested, saying that he could help, Jack and the others refused, telling him that he was needed elsewhere. He went with one of the groups to a safe house, helping to keep everyone in order and from panicking too much.

Finally, with the house empty, the cold morning air blowing up against their forms, nipping at the tiny exposed areas of flesh, Jack, Maria, Jill and Paul—the four chosen for the mission—set out to the bridge. Maria protested quietly to Jack, telling him that Jill was not stable enough to come along.

"You have something you need to tell me?" he asked.

Maria rolled her eyes. "Leave it be for now. I just don't want her around."

"We need fast, able bodies in case the plan goes awry. She's a former athlete, and as much as I like Duane, he'd older and agreed that he'd only slow us down. He's better off serving as a guard for one of the groups."

"Fine," Maria agreed, then told Jack what had happened during the escape.

"She killed Susan? Even after you told her we had a cure?"

Maria nodded. "The girl may be athletic and want to kill the undead," she tapped the side of her head, "but she's not quite right upstairs."

"We'll keep an eye on her, but for now, we need her."

With that, the four gathered outside, ready to ride out Jack's plan.

CHAPTER 25

Paul drove the Suburban. Chains had been secured to the tires, making the vehicle a beast in the snow. Jack sat in the passenger seat, bouncing up and down every time the chains collided with the pavement, the linked loops of steels chewing through the white stuff with ease. Jill was behind him in the second row. Jack could tell from the short time he'd been around her that she had some serious issues and was a complete hard-ass. She was young, had been through a lot, but she was tough and fearless too. Perfect for what had to be done.

Maria took up the rear, watching the road from behind, a Remington 750 semi-automatic rifle at the ready. The going was slow, the roads slippery, but the truck did all right. No one spoke as the group made its way down the mountain. Unplowed streets, not a single set of tire tracks, were simply a strange and unsettling sight. If there were other people about, there was no sign of them. The good news was that it also meant Cannibal hadn't arrived yet.

They reached the bridge blockade thirty minutes after leaving the house. Paul killed the engine and everyone exited the vehicle. After listening to the chains' jingle-like cadence, the silence was eerie.

The wind was fiercest down by the water, bringing an immediate chill to the survivors. Maria, Jill and Jack took up position around the SUV, keeping watch on the perimeter. Paul was familiar with using Front-End loaders, having driven the huge yellow monsters before. He fired up the tractor, smoke billowing upwards from the black exhaust pipe poking from the machine's boxy rear.

One by one, Paul began pushing, sometimes rolling the staircase of vehicles out of the way. A lot of noise was made—the machine's roaring engine and the crunch and scrape of metal as the vehicles were shoved into a muddled pile. The ruckus was all part of the plan. They would need as many of the undead on the bridge as possible.

With the wall-of-vehicles' support gone, the structure wouldn't be nearly as stable. Jack peered through a partially crushed pickup truck's window and saw that hundreds of undead had made their way over to the blockade, with more coming. The sound of a rifle shot caused him to spin around. About thirty feet out lay a body. From the woods to the left, two more undead were making their way over to the group. Maria and Jill fired their rifles, each woman hitting their mark. It was figured that any undead nearby would come from the hillside, but Jack had hoped the number would be manageable, at least until the crux of what they needed to do was underway, then it wouldn't matter much.

Now came the tricky part of the plan—getting the wall of vehicles to come down so that the zombies would be able to pour out like liquid, and not in a single file line. They needed a horde.

Paul parked the loader off to the side next to a bulldozer and joined Jack at the SUV. Maria and Jill kept picking off any undead that came too close. Jack and Paul grabbed propane tanks fitted with fuses and placed them in the car-wall, spacing them both high and low. All the fuses were then tied to a single fuse, which Paul lit. It was figured they had about five minutes.

Everyone hopped in the SUV, which drove about a hundred feet away before stopping.

The explosion was ground shaking. Four of the ten propane tanks went off at the same time, the others seconds later, obliterating the entire middle section of the wall. Pieces of twisted metal and plastic cascaded the area, kicking up snow and debris. Cars that hadn't taken much damage tilted and tumbled down, crashing to the sides or into the river.

Everyone in the truck cheered.

As the smoke cleared, Jack saw the first of the undead appear from the wreckage. He imagined a large number were destroyed, but the explosion itself would only attract more. The wind picked up, quickly blowing the smoke away. Jack's eyes widened at the horrific sight as an army of undead came through.

"Now," he said.

Maria opened the rear doors and began firing into the horde. The zombies would now have a target.

"Wait until they're close, then we move," Jack shouted.

Within minutes, the roadway was filled with rotting corpses, each one coming for the truck. Paul drove slowly, keeping just ahead of the throng. Maria didn't need to fire the weapon anymore, the meals-on-wheels locked to the zombies' sights.

Just before reaching the incline that led to the mountain road, Paul stopped the truck. He waited until the undead were within a few feet, then took off; getting enough momentum to make sure he made it up the hill. The tires spun. The truck slowed. "Come on, Baby," Paul said, giving it gas, "come on." The truck continued to climb, the undead along with it. Some stumbled, falling into each other, but the hill wasn't very steep, most able to ascend.

Finally, the SUV reached the road and Paul steered into the previous tracks. The SUV jumped forward. Paul hit the brakes and Jack crashed into the windshield, Jill and Maria into the backs of their seats.

"Seatbelts, people," Paul said, having his on.

The SUV continued up the road at a slow pace, the chains on the tires making the go easy. Heavy snow started to fall, the large, close-together flakes making it difficult to see in the distance. Maria had pointed out that parts of the road leading up the mountain could be seen from the deck at Cannibal's place.

"I figured that might be the case," Jack said. "If someone notices an army of undead coming up the road, then so be it; nothing we can do about it. But with so many zombies, I don't think it will matter."

"Unless Cannibal's men meet us before we get to his house," Paul said. "A firefight, with the undead so close behind us, would surely be bad. We'd be chow, or trapped in this tin can which would be riddled with bullets in no time, and the undead might never reach their intended destination."

Silence followed the statement. Jack swallowed hard, the lump in his throat a psychological manifestation of failure. If they met resistance along the way, the plan was finished, but there was nothing anyone could do about it now. Jack had to hope Maria's assessment of Cannibal's crew being lackluster and lazy was true.

He stared straight ahead, trying to catch any signs of trouble that might be coming their way.

The undead followed at a steady pace, pushing through the white stuff, never showing any sign they were cold or tired. The parade of the bot-controlled corpses was incredible, awesome and frightening at the same time.

With each passing minute, Jack feared they would run into Cannibal's men, the former inmates on their way to meet them, the undead, or to attack Cliff House. But an hour later, Jack and the crew were on the road that led to Cannibal's place with no sign of opposition. The going was slow, but necessary in order to keep the undead following.

As the SUV bounced along slowly, Jack felt his anxiety level rise. They were getting close to the targeted area. Maria had said there were no guards, but Jack found that hard to believe. Even the most lax, overconfident fortifications would have some form of watch. And now that there had been multiple escapes, Cannibal would want to make sure his kingdom was secure.

With the snow continuing to fall, the flakes large and puffy like balls of cotton, seeing more than ten feet ahead was difficult.

"I think we're getting close," Paul said. "I've been watching the mileage meter. It can't be much farther ahead."

Jack saw what looked like three figures up ahead. He looked through a pair of binoculars Paul had in the truck. It wasn't three armed men, but four. The road around them was plowed. It had to be where the driveway was located.

"Stop here," Jack said. "This is our stop."

"You sure?" Paul asked.

"Yes."

The original plan was to head down the driveway all the way to the house, then let the undead do their thing as Jack and the others sauntered away, but things changed.

Everyone hopped out of the vehicle, Paul turning off the engine. Jack and the others opened fire at the men down the road, knowing they probably weren't going to hit anything. Cannibal's men returned fire, a few bullets pinging off the truck.

"Now," Jack said. He and the others took off for the woods. They scampered up the hill and waited just off the road. Cannibal's men, unable to see much, kept firing.

The undead were coming, their putrid odor carried ahead of them by the wind. They passed right by the SUV, going around it as if it were nothing more than a natural landmark, heading toward the sound of weapons fire.

Jack couldn't help but smile, his plan was working perfectly.

CHAPTER 26

Cannibal was awoken by a harsh knocking on his door. He hated being stirred from a sound sleep, preferring to wake when his body was ready to do so. Whoever it was might become dinner, unless the reason for the intrusion was a good one.

"Come in," he shouted, sitting up and wiping the tiredness from his face.

He needed his men for the upcoming assault on Cliff House—which should have happened already if not for his soldiers being unorganized pieces of mindless flesh sacks. Wastes. Once he had control over his children, he wouldn't need *man* anymore, save for the meals they would become for him and his children.

He foresaw the future. People were herded like cattle, made to breed and serve the undead and their father. It would all take time, but it would begin soon. He felt it in his soul. The power of the flesh he was eating was bringing him closer to ultimate power. Soon he'd be able to command his flock and take over the world. Cooking flesh would no longer be necessary; he would eat it raw like his children did.

"Sir," a man named Gile said, "the bridge . . . the wall . . . the undead . . ."

"Spit it out," Cannibal groaned.

"Stilts was on patrol," the man said, breathing heavily, "and saw that the blockade on the bridge was blown open. He thought he heard something this morning, but was unsure. Once it was light out, he took a look and saw it—an army of undead coming up the mountain."

Was this it? Cannibal wondered. Were his children coming to him? He had been feeling ready, as if any day now he'd be the king of the undead, the father they needed.

"There was also a vehicle in front of them," the man continued, "a black SUV. It was moving slow, just keeping out of the zombies' reach. Stilts lost sight of it though."

This was odd, Cannibal thought. First the escape. Cable missing. Now this. He'd feared Cable was taken hostage, but none of the men had seen Cable with the escapees. Now a vehicle was seen leading the undead. There was just too much going on. Too much of the unknown. For all Cannibal knew, Cable was leading the undead to him. A shiver ran down his spine. Truth be told, he wasn't sure if he was ready yet. He'd felt something, but . . .

"Get the men ready," he ordered. "Send a squad of four immediately out to the road. Make sure they do not engage the undead. If they see them, tell them to report back here. I want everyone else to take up arms and be ready to defend our home."

"Defend?" the man asked. "Against who?"

"Just do it," Cannibal roared.

The man nodded, turned, and ran out the door.

CHAPTER 27

Stilts and three others were told to grab some weapons and head out to the road. They were ordered not to shoot any undead. Regardless, each man took as powerful a weapon as they could find. Orders were orders, but if those rotting things came too close, all bets were off.

They hurried up the driveway to the road, a few of the men having plowed it last night with the pickup truck. The falling snow was going to make it difficult to get a decent view of the road in the distance, but it was what it was.

Stilts had spent most of his adult life behind bars. This newest bout of freedom looked like it was going to last awhile, maybe for the remainder of his days. The world was a whole new ball game now, one he much preferred. He knew next to nothing about technology—cell phones, computers, cars, etc. Sure, a person could read about that stuff, but who had the time? He was always busy watching his back or the backs of his friends.

If he'd gotten out when the world was operating at normalcy, he'd be useless. He would wind up right back in the slammer for sure. Prison kept people in the past and this new world was more past than present. He'd been so worried that when he got out he'd be like a forgotten relic. He had no family, at least none that wanted anything to do with him.

In fact, prison had prepared him for this harsh world. He'd been living most of his life with eyes in the back of his head. Taking what was his, learning to trust no one. Survival of the fittest. This new world didn't give a shit about law and order. There were no guards to keep the peace, no police to call. Now it was "take care of business, take care of yourself", and that was just the way he liked it. The world was the criminal's playground, as far as he was concerned.

Cannibal was a sick fuck, no doubt, but he was a leader and had saved all of their asses. The men feared him; obeyed him. That might change one day, but for now, he was the boss. Stilts didn't like that most of the women brought in were only for Cannibal, the men not allowed to touch them. But on occasion, the boss man gave one over to the men to do as they pleased with, which was way more than Stilts had ever gotten on the inside—at least from a female. For now, like all other things, Stilts followed the rules.

Along with carnal pleasures, there was plenty of alcohol and guns to go around. What more could a man ask for? If it wasn't for the undead, he'd have thought he had died and gone to Heaven, or maybe he was in his kind of Hell.

Stilts and the other men, Stench, Mack, and Heathen made it to the road, and after fifteen minutes, relaxed a bit, thinking nothing was going to happen. They bullshitted and complained, smoked cigarettes and weed, a boatload of the green stuff having been swiped from the State Trooper barracks.

Snow continued to fall in clumps. The air was colder in the morning, but somehow refreshing too. It unnerved him to know so many of the undead were now traipsing around the mountainside. Hopefully they weren't coming to the house. The blown bridge blockade would mean more patrols, which meant less down time. Even with all their weapons, he didn't know if they'd be able to stop them.

"Fucking freezing out here," Stench said. Stench was a smelly bastard. He hardly showered when he was in prison, the guards had to force him, which was what he wanted. He was gang raped up in Attica and had a fear of showers ever since. At least when the guards were present, he felt safe. It was strange because he hated the guards, had sent one to the ICU for calling his momma a dirty whore. Stilts couldn't figure the man out.

"Yeah, it's too cold to be outside, standing around," said Mack, rubbing his arms through his coat. "If there is an army of zombies heading our way, what are we supposed to do? Just run back and tell everyone? We can't fire on them, and what would be the point? There's so damn many of them."

Heathen lit a cigarette. "I see any of those fuckers, I'm shooting."

"We've got orders and we'll follow them," Stilts said, making sure he caught the eye of every convict.

He didn't mind the cold. It was the heat he disliked. In prison, it was always so damn hot in the summer. It was worth getting hurt just to be able to visit the air-conditioned infirmary.

"You hear that?" Heathen asked.

"Yeah," said Stilts. "An engine. Chained tires."

"Snow tires?" Mack asked.

The four men glared down the road. Stilts couldn't see much, but it looked like a vehicle was heading their way. Some survivors looking for a place to hole up?

The ca-chunk, ca-chunk from the chains colliding against pavement ceased, the engine going quiet.

"What do we do?" Heathen asked.

"Boss man didn't say anything about firing on people," Mack said.

"Think they saw us?" Stench asked.

"I can barely see them, but it's possible," Stilts said. "Let's see what—"

Shots rang out as people exited the vehicle. Stilts and the others returned fire. Motherfuckers were going to pay, he thought. He pulled the trigger as rapidly as possible; hoping the spray from all their rounds combined would do some nice damage.

Gunfire filled the air as the four men stood practically shoulder-to-shoulder unloading hell on their attackers. Finally, when their weapons needed reloading, Stilts realized they weren't being fired upon anymore. "Hold it," he said, ears ringing. All was quiet in the land of snow.

"I think we got them," Heathen said.

"We'll have to go check it . . ." his mouth dropped open. A wave of darkness was coming down the road. The others saw it too.

"What the hell is that?" Mack asked.

It took a moment for Stilts' brain to compute the image, then he knew. The undead had found them. The whole thing was a trick to lure them here. It was why the group from the truck had stopped firing. They weren't dead; they were off in the woods, hiding.

"Holy shit," Stench said, and opened fire. The other men followed suit. The undead drew closer; their bodies crumbling under the hail of bullets, but the ones that went down were replaced by others, the horde getting nearer.

"Fuck this," Mack said, "I'm out of here."

The man was correct. There was no point in staying here. Thanks to the gunfire, the undead had their new target, no longer the vehicle that led them here. Stilts and the others followed Mack up the driveway. They ran hard, hoping the undead would pass them by and head on down the road. When Stilts turned back, the driveway was tranquil, and for a moment, he breathed a sigh of relief. But then he saw the first of numerous undead come around the corner.

"Shit, we're fucked."

CHAPTER 28

Jack and the others sat huddled in the woods, watching the undead march by. The wind gusted, blowing the snow around in blizzard-like effect. He squinted against the cold, his eyes tearing.

The stench from the undead was overpowering, settling over the group like some unseen veil of putrid-ness. Everyone except Jill had pulled their jackets up over their noses, the act doing little to quell the stench.

Jill had a look of malice in her eyes, and watched the undead like a lion in wait. She was trembling, but it wasn't from the cold or fear. It was from anger. Jack could tell by the look on her face. He tapped her arm. "Are you okay?" he whispered.

She looked at him and nodded, the fierceness in her expression remained unchanged.

Jack wasn't sure he believed her. He feared she might lose it. He didn't know her, *really* know her. She might be crazy enough to go charging down the hill. He remembered what Maria had told him; how Jill had killed that poor girl, a person she'd spent time getting to know. And she'd done it without a second thought. She refused to believe him and the others even now about how an infected person could be cured. The people of Cliff House took their word for it, but not Jill. The girl was too damaged.

Maybe it was better she didn't know the truth, at least for now, because when she did, it might just push her farther down the going-insane trail to full-on insane.

When the undead mob-train finally ended, the group worked its way down to the road. Gunshots rang out in the distance and Jack realized his plan had worked. The undead were at Cannibal's house. Ammo would be used in great quantity. Men would die. Soon it would be time for stage two.

The SUV had taken damage. The grill and headlights were busted up. The windshield was cracked and littered with bullet holes. The leather seats were shredded and the back window was blown out, but the tires were intact and the engine turned over. Steam began coming from the hood a mile down the road, but the truck made it to one of the rendezvous houses regardless.

"How'd it go?" Don asked, meeting Jack outside.

"Couldn't have gone better."

Don shook his head slowly, smiling. "Unbelievable."

Jack and the others went inside. They rested and warmed up by the fire, drank hot beverages and ate a meal. Sentries were posted outside and gunshots could be heard off in the distance, the war at Cannibal's was going strong. For once, Jack rooted for the zombies.

Cannibal hadn't felt real fear in a very long time, but the unwanted sensation was with him now. The undead, his future children, were attacking the house, killing his men. He'd given orders not to engage the rotting corpses, but that apparently didn't matter. He'd hated having to entrust and work with such degenerates, but what choice did he have? The truth was, he was a loner, never to be understood. An evolved being, and unfortunately needed to rely on society's scum.

Sitting in his chair, behind a locked door, Cannibal decided to wait out the inevitable. Doubt ran rampant through his mind. The dead were here to follow or perhaps kill him—if he wasn't ready. But it was his destiny to lead them and to rule over the land. He'd known he was special since he was a little boy and ate his neighbor's dog. He was reborn that day, becoming the man he was now—everything leading up to this moment. He was Cannibal, the one the demons talked to and told the truth. The one who would control the undead. Doubt was being pushed out by assuredness. He had nothing to fear, they were here for him, not to eat, but to be led. His men were no longer needed, their gunshots dwindling over time as the undead broke through the ranks and into the house.

Cannibal threw his .45 to the floor and marched over to the door. He could smell the rancid aroma of his children on the other side of the door, waiting for him to make his appearance. Without wasting another moment, he unlocked and opened the door.

"My children," he said, stepping out into the living room, the place swarming with zombies. Men from the balcony were blasting away at them, heads being obliterated. Anger coursed through Cannibal's veins. "Get them, my children. Kill them all."

Two zombies closest to him made their way over. Cannibal stared at them, confused, not seeing any signs of recognition in their eyes. "Go save your brothers and sisters," Cannibal ordered, pointing in the other direction. Three more undead joined the two heading toward Cannibal.

No, he thought. He will not fear them. They are only coming to serve.

The first two zombies reached him. They reached out and clawed at his flesh, collapsing in on him. Panic seized the big man as he flung them off. "No, what are you doing? I'm your father!" The zombies rose to their feet and came forward, now seven in total. They encircled Cannibal. He punched and kicked a few, but the numbers overwhelmed him and soon he was being bitten and torn apart. He felt his right ear rip free. He howled as a finger caught on his lip. The skin stretched until it snapped, blood spurting forth. Pain erupted across his legs and stomach as mouths began to feed. Finally the man fell, a mass of undead descending on him. He screamed in agony as fingers and mouths took his flesh, his eyes exploding as nails pierced them. Darkness falling over him, he could still feel, and the pain lasted for what seemed like hours until finally he went numb and knew no more.

Hours later, the gunshots lessened until there was none at all.

A side had won.

Everyone at the safe house gathered their weapons and climbed into vehicles, SUVs and one of the armored trucks. They made their way over to Cannibal's house, stopping along the road just before the driveway. They exited the vehicles. The air was noiseless save for the howling winds, like unseen banshees from a local bog.

Three groups, consisting of four people each, were formed. Jack, Paul, Jill and Maria made their way up the driveway, taking the most direct route. The others headed into the woods, planning to approach the house from different angles.

The silence was eerie, the crunch of hardened snow underfoot seeming to equal the rumble of thunder. The house was viewable through the sparsely leaved trees, but until they came around the bend in the driveway, the real horrors were not revealed.

Hundreds of bodies lay about like something from a Civil War scene except here corpses were barely recognizable. The smell from the road was putrid enough, but up close, the odor was unbearable. The rotted corpses were shredded and torn apart by bullets. Some of the undead were struggling to move, but the lack of limbs made the simple task impossible. A few were pulling themselves along, their lower extremities having been blown off. Anything that came near the group was quickly put down with a single shot to the head. Arms, legs, heads and torsos were caught on the branches or wedged between them in the surrounding trees. The whole scene looked as if a bomb had gone off. The reek of death and rot was overwhelming.

Jack kicked away a fleshy jawbone as he surveyed the area for signs of life, but found none. Inside, people might still be alive. The garage doors were gone, broken through by the horde. Like grain coming from a tipped-over broken sack, the undead spilled from the garage, laid out and toppled amongst each other. There was no way he and the others were entering through there.

They headed to the front of the house. Jack tried opening the windowless double doors with no success. Gunshots sounded from within. "Stand back," he said, before pointing his 12 gauge Remington at the lock and firing. It took two blasts before the door was able to open. He pushed to get in, but found that something was blocking the door from opening all the way. Peering inside, he saw a number of bodies on the floor. He shoved harder and was able to open the door farther, sliding two of the corpses out of the way.

The others followed suit.

The walls of the foyer were littered with bullet holes and gore. Undead bodies lay motionless—truly dead, along with a former inmate, the flesh on his face half eaten away, but the rest of him looking in decent shape. Jack pulled his .45 and put a bullet into the corpse's head.

A wide, red-carpeted staircase that led to the second floor was draped with fallen figures. The marble banister was missing chunks and fractured throughout, resembling some ancient Greek structure from long ago.

The scrape and clatter of shuffling feet sounded from one of the rooms down the hall. Two zombies appeared, one missing its right arm. The wounds—scratches and bite marks—along their flesh were glistening with red. They weren't bridge-zombies. Jack recognized one of them as a Cannibal lackey. Impossible, he thought—the bots took at least a day to reanimate a corpse. He aimed the .45 and put a bullet into each one's head.

"Those were Cannibal's men," Maria said, as if reading his mind.

"Yeah. I guess the bots figured out a way to turn people faster. No way to know whether they were infected while they were alive and were killed quickly by the things, or died from a gunshot wound, and then came back. Either way, the bots have gotten stronger."

The group stuck together. Jack was in the lead, heading down the hallway that led to the basement, and living room beyond. He stepped over corpses and around body parts, most of them undead, but some from the recently deceased. Anything without its brains blown out received a bullet to the head. Some of the corpses were riddled with bite marks, pieces of flesh torn away.

He passed by the basement door with a feeling of disgust in his gut, remembering how he and the others were kept locked up. Each room along the hallway was checked—nothing but dead bodies everywhere. The last stop was the living room, a place where corpses were practically piled on top of each other. Jack wanted to make this quick, then leave the place. The smells and visuals were both things he wanted to be far away from as soon as possible.

Gunfire erupted from the balcony overhead. Jack dove back into the hallway. Jill scrambled behind a sofa. Paul and Maria hugged the wall just underneath the balcony, and appeared to be out of the shooter's line of sight.

"Stop firing," Jack yelled, not knowing what else to say.

"Fuck you," the voice answered. Bullets riddled the floor in front of him. Then the man shot all over the place, including at the sofa Jill was using to hide behind. "I'll kill you all."

A noise from behind caught Jack's attention. He turned and saw Stilts, the extremely tall, rat-faced bastard, come from the basement. Their eyes met. Stilts went to raise his weapon.

Jack was faster with the .45. He fired twice, the first bullet clipping the lanky man's over-sized right ear, the second hitting its mark. Stilts' right eye disappeared as the bullet entered the socket, then exited out the back of his head, caking the walls with gore. Stilts fell back, hit the doorframe and tumbled down the stairs.

"Jack," Maria yelled from the living room.

"I'm fine," he said.

"Fucking die," the man in the balcony yelled, continuing to fire his weapon.

A male voice cried out.

A single shot went off, but it wasn't from the balcony-shooter.

"What's going on?" Jack asked.

"Paul's been bitten," Maria said.

Jack thought he heard wrong, but with all the dead bodies around maybe one made its way over to them and they didn't notice it with the man shooting at them. If Paul had been bitten, then Jack needed to get the man to safety—and fast. With Cannibal's men having turned so quickly, Paul might not have much time.

Jack bolted down the hallway and back to the foyer, then up the staircase, hopping over the bodies in his path. At the top of the stairs, amongst a pile of corpses, a female zombie grabbed his foot, tripping Jack up. He crashed into the wall, then righted himself and spun around. He met the crawling, legless, faceless thing and brought a boot down on its head repeatedly until it stopped moving.

He headed down a hallway, passing by a number of unoccupied bedrooms before finally reaching the balcony. He hugged the wall, making sure the shooter wouldn't be able to see him should the man turn around.

"I can wait here all day," Balcony Man said, firing off a few more rounds. "I got food and water. You people are as good as dead unless you leave me alone."

Jack moved slowly, avoiding the fragments of broken glass and sheetrock. The shooter was facing away, leaning over the terrace.

"Drop it," Jack said.

The man flinched, but remained where he was.

"Drop it or I'll drop you," Jack demanded. He could have easily blown the guy away, but there was something unsettling about shooting a man, even a scumbag, in the back.

Jack heard the rifle crash to the floor below. The man put his arms up and turned around. His nose was crooked and split across the bridge. Blood trickled from the wound, the man's beard caked with crimson. He had beady eyes, the pupils little more than pinpricks.

"I got the shooter," Jack yelled. Then to the man, "Let's go." He almost hoped the guy would try something, giving him the excuse to shoot him dead. But the man didn't do anything except obey Jack's commands. He kept his hands on his head and walked down the hall to the stairs, then on to the living room from there—Jack keeping his gun pointed at him the entire time.

The scene downstairs wasn't a good one. Jill was pointing her weapon at Paul. Maria had her M4 trained on Jill.

Balcony Man started laughing. Not wanting to deal with more than a single issue, Jack hit the man on the back of the neck with the butt of his .45 and knocked him out.

"Jill," he said, "put the gun away; we have more pressing concerns right now."

Paul's left pant leg was torn and bloody. Jill's gun arm was steady, her eyes focused on Paul's.

"I told you we shouldn't have brought this crazy bitch along," Maria said.

"Everyone relax." Jack holstered his weapon. "Jill, put the gun away. If you shoot Paul, you'll be killing an innocent man and it'll be the last thing you ever do."

"He's going to die miserably," Jill said through clenched teeth. "You people want him to suffer? I've seen what happens."

"So have we," Jack said. "My wife was infected and killed. If I'd only known what I know now I could've saved her. We can save Paul. You have to believe me. Don't do this."

Maria stepped up. "I'd lower your weapon now if I were you."

"You people are fucked up. Cruel." Jill lowered her gun and stepped away. "Keep him the hell away from me."

"We still got a house to clear," Jack said, tugging on Maria's arm, getting her mind back to the job at hand.

"Paul needs help," she said, then faced Jill. "I'll tell you what, how about *you* stay the hell away from us."

"When he turns and infects someone else, don't say I didn't warn you," Jill said.

"How many times do we have to tell you that we can cure people? Get it through your thick skull. Do you think we're making this shit up?"

Jill walked out of the room. Jack saw tears welling in her eyes.

"Where are you going?" he asked.

"Somewhere else."

"Let her be, Jack," Maria said. "This place still isn't secure."

They made their way upstairs and looked around until they found the weapons room. As Jack had hoped, the tasers were there, along with Zaun's sword. They zapped Paul twice, hoping it would still do the trick, then wrapped his leg in a strip of cloth.

The prisoner was tied up and left in the trophy room. They went through the rest of the house, meeting up with Don and the others who had come in at the far end. Undead milled about here and there, but were quickly put down. What remained of Cannibal's corpse was found inside his room of horror—a human-bone chair at the center. Three zombies were still gnawing on the big man's flesh.

Once the house was cleared, the prisoner was brought outside. Weapons and any salvageable supplies were gathered. The weapon room was a good find, the place still stocked with plenty of guns and ammo.

A few hours later, the snow had picked up again, covering the bodies and carnage. Gasoline was brought in and the house was lit up. The corpses outside were piled together and set afire.

Everyone, including Jill and the prisoner, traveled back to Cliff House. Two vehicles were dispatched to the rendezvous houses to let the people know it was safe to return home.

That night, especially with no casualties taken, the people of Cliff House celebrated. Wine and alcohol flowed, food was prepared and eaten. Full bellies were aplenty. Jack was happy to see the people of Cliff House smile again. They deserved one night of escape, of living. Through his meandering about, talking with folk, getting numerous thank yous and pats on the back, he found Jill in the kitchen, alone. She was sitting in a chair, her back to him, looking out the window at the gloomy night.

"I need you to come with me," Jack said.

Jill remained in her chair. "I heard Paul's fine. I guess you people know what you're talking about. The plague is curable, nothing more than tiny robots."

"That's what I wanted to show you. Paul's well. He's in the living room, talking and having a good time."

"Yes. Good for him . . . I saw him earlier. From a distance. He looked good."

Jack thought about going over to her, but decided to leave her be. Some people needed time alone to figure things out. "Don't be too hard on yourself. You've been through a lot; seen horrors we thought were only in books and movies. Knowledge is power and now you have more. Move forward. If you want to talk, come find me. I'll be around."

Jack turned and left the room.

CHAPTER 29

Jill heard Jack's retreating footsteps. She almost laughed—*Jack and Jill went up the hill . . .*

She looked down at the gun in her lap, a .357 Colt revolver. Her grin fell. She had found it amongst one of the dead inmates, promptly tucking into her pants. No one had seen her take it. With the way people had been acting, she felt she needed it. Jack, Maria . . . hell all of them were nuts.

After arriving back at the house, she finally talked to some of the others. They believed the bot story and how there was a cure, that cure being voltage, electricity. Jack, Maria and Zaun, their epic, incredible, heart-of-the-epidemic-story was true. She hadn't doubted what they went through, but an underground bunker? Secret military experiment? The infected were curable? Jack's plan, as improbable as it seemed at first, had worked. So after listening to the people of Cliff House and then seeing the proof of Paul's recovery, she had no choice but to believe everything about the three survivors.

No one but the people involved knew what she did to the girl in the woods, to Susan, and no one but the people there knew what she tried to do at Cannibal's house with Paul. They'd kept it to themselves. They were honorable people.

She had been angry with them, hoping Paul would get sick, turn and attack them. Then she'd show them, tell them how stupid they were. But Paul got better. The guy had never even reached any visible stages of infection. How could she have become so cynical? Hoping to see someone fall ill to make a point. Hoping in that sense was not right, but hoping in the positive sense proved fatal in her world. She'd lost her whole family relying on hope. She'd made a promise never to let anyone suffer like they had.

She'd visited the infirmary after getting back to the house. Shock sticks had been made—pieces of metal hooked up to car batteries, the voltage made to equal that of the tasers. These people hadn't laughed Jack and his friends off when they found out. Instead, they believed and made a tool.

Jill shook with rage. She'd seen so many people die, but it was her family that pushed her over the edge, made her cold. All they needed was a little electricity. Why didn't the government warn people? All that was said was to "remain in your homes until further notice." There was never further notice.

Tears streamed down Jill's cheeks. She grabbed the gun and held it. It felt so heavy. Her arm grew tired. She'd killed that poor girl, Susan. Murdered her. She'd gotten to know her, about her family, where she was from. They were even friends, right? There was no way Jill could've known she'd be okay after she was bitten. Up until that point, everyone that had been bitten died. Became monsters. She was doing Susan a favor.

Jill had run into others along her journey though. She'd killed them too, knowing what was in store for them. Some had been very sick, on the brink of turning, but not all. Some looked okay, maybe a little pale, sickly, but very much alive. It was the bite marks that proved they were nothing more than dead people walking and gave her the right to end their suffering.

Murderer.

But was she? She was only using the information she had at the time. Doing what she thought was right, and by no means easy. Those people would've died miserably—well, all except Susan. If she'd listened to Maria, Susan could've been here at Cliff House, talking and laughing. Breathing.

Jill's sadness was erased by sudden anger. How could she even think about killing herself? She needed to survive. It's what her family would have wanted. She was a good person. Not a murderer. The government was the problem. They should've been on the ball.

She realized she had something important to do, to help people. Cure people. Inform people. Use the new knowledge to combat this man-made plague.

Or she could end it all and not have to carry around the guilt she felt.

CHAPTER 30

The next morning, after a hearty breakfast of deer meat, juice and coffee, Jack, Maria and Zaun packed up and set out to leave. The three survivors had sorted through the plundered bounty that had been Cannibal's arsenal. All in all, along with the M4 Maria had already acquired during the escape from Cannibal's, the two remaining M4 machine guns and tasers were found, along with Jack's Mossberg 12 gauge, but not his Sig Sauer 9 mm. At least he had his original Smith and Wesson .45. He still couldn't believe the first man he killed back at that house when he was running for his life had been using *his* .45, as if the gun truly belonged with him. Zaun and Maria grabbed a couple of Glock 9 mm's. Maria kept, with Don's permission of course, the Remington 750, wanting a long-range weapon in case the need arrived. A number of goodbyes were exchanged, a few tears were shared, but it was smiles all around.

Don, Paul and Duane stood outside in the driveway opposite Jack and the others. Two Polaris snowmobiles were set out, fueled up, and ready to go.

"I can't thank you enough for the sleds," Jack said to Don.

"I wish we could do more," Don replied. "The people of Cliff House will forever be grateful to you all." Don shook each of their hands. Paul and Duane followed suit.

"At anytime," Don continued, "whatever happens in this world, please feel free to stop by or call upon us should you need anything."

"Let's hope the next time we meet," Maria said, "this whole plague-thing is finished."

"Amen to that," Duane said.

Jill came from the house. She had a backpack on and looked ready to travel.

She walked up to the gathering. "Can I talk to you, Jack?"

"Sure."

"Actually," she said, "I need to talk to all of you." She took a moment, then looked at Maria. "I'm sorry. I'm sorry for the things I did, and the way I acted."

Maria said nothing, only nodded.

"I've learned a lot over the last couple of days. I have a new view on the world and I feel I have a duty to perform now. I want to help people. Spread the word about the bot-epidemic. I want to come with you guys."

Don's eyebrows shot up.

Jack was taken aback. He didn't know what to say. "Don't you want to stay here, be a part of Cliff House?"

She looked at Don and smiled. "I like it here, but it's not for me." To Jack, "I need to be out there, helping people, killing the undead. The information about the plague is too important. I'll come with you, help you guys in any way possible. And if it comes to it, I'll go out on my own to keep spreading the cure."

Jack turned to Maria. She shrugged. "As long as she doesn't slow us down, and promises to do as we ask . . ."

"Fine with me," Zaun said.

"Okay, Jill," Jack said. "Welcome aboard."

The girl smiled warmly, then hugged him and Maria at the same time, pulling them in tightly.

After a few more goodbyes, the group climbed onto their snowmobiles and headed down the driveway and onto the road.

CHAPTER 31

Cable situated himself on the second floor of a two-story strip mall that was located along the Thruway, opposite the Palisades Mall, a grand, four-story galleria. The pain was almost gone from his chest, that Zaun character did some job on him. Just two days ago, he'd been on his way north, ready to forget about Cannibal, Jack and all the others, but then something extraordinary happened.

He'd acquired a snowmobile from one of the local residences. Knowing that leaving the area was a wise decision, he headed down to the highway, aware the snowmobile would be able to get him wherever he wished to travel—of which he had no clue.

The wind was gusting, blowing drifts of snow across the road and cars. Cable hated running, especially when he had unfinished business—Jack. Zaun had beaten him fairly, but Jack hadn't. But to stay around could prove his downfall.

Sitting there, facing north along the Thruway, Cable was startled by an explosion, one he not only heard clearly, but felt in his bones. It came from behind, down by the bridge. Interest peaked and with no destination in mind, he turned the sled around and headed south.

He stopped before reaching the overpass that ran over the Thruway just before the bridge. From his position, he was hidden from the bridge and anyone that might be there. Killing the sled's engine, he proceeded on foot, rifle slung over his shoulder. He trudged through the snow, entered the overpasses underneath and hugged the wall, creeping along it until he reached the end.

Peering out, he saw a black SUV moving slowly across the highway. The wall of cars had been blown open, the undead pouring out. A parade of zombies was following the vehicle. He saw Jack through the passenger window. When the SUV reached the hill, it went up and he saw Maria sitting in the rear.

It took a moment to consider the scene, and then it hit him. Jack and his companions were geniuses. No wonder the man had eluded him back at the house and in the forest. Cable had underestimated him, Zaun as well, to a degree.

They were leading the dead up the mountain, no doubt to Cannibal's place, like the Pied Piper of legend. This was most unexpected and intriguing. He couldn't leave now, not without seeing if this most dangerous, incredible plan was going to work.

He headed back to his sled and then made his way up the mountain through the woods and backroads until he reached a place that allowed him a view of the Cannibal house. But it wasn't enough, so he scrambled down through the woods, and to a position just off the road where he saw four of Cannibal's men. They were standing around, each holding a rifle.

Before long, a gun battle broke out, which was clearly a ruse to get the dead to follow Cannibal's men to the house.

Cable grinned to himself, glad he made the decision to leave when he did. Looks like Cliff House was the winner. Jack and his friends were simply too interesting to leave behind. He'd never be able to forget about them, and since he had nowhere to go, he decided to make Jack and the others a part of his life, at least until he killed them or they killed him.

Now, he was approximately four miles north of the Tappan Zee Bridge, far enough to make sure his friends wouldn't make it back to Cliff House on foot, should they choose that path. They would be taken off guard, frightened and most likely look to dig in somewhere. Maybe the mall? That would be a great hunting ground, he thought.

Cable was taking a gamble though. He had no idea when Jack and his companions would leave Cliff House or if they'd even come his way. He figured since they came from the city, they wouldn't head back there, let alone south—so north it had to be. The Thruway was the only main artery for miles around and the easiest route. Odds were in his favor, but waiting for them might prove difficult. He had limited supplies and it was cold, his little fire keeping him warm, but if a blizzard came through, he'd be in for a tough time.

He'd wait a week, if they didn't show, then he'd have to forget about them and move on. He remained awake throughout the day, feeling comfortable about sleeping at night, figuring no one would dare travel during that time.

He awoke early the next morning, both the military and prison conditioning his internal clock, and climbed onto the roof where he'd cleared an area, and waited.

Two hours later, he heard the sound of multiple high-pitched engines. He peered through the scope of the Browning 300 and saw the first of two snowmobiles. They were moving at a decent pace up the roadway. The noise had attracted a few undead from the area.

Each sled had two passengers. Jack's group had three. Cable wondered if this was a different party, or maybe Jack's group had picked up a fourth? It appeared from the type of outfits and hair whipping around from the helmets that each machine had a male and female member, though Cable could not be certain.

He had a decision to make: act, and hope these were his targets, or let them go and hope Jack and the others hadn't come along yet. Then he saw the Samurai sword. It was strapped to a rider's back. Excitement coursed through Cable, his fingertips igniting with electricity. His lips curled into a smile.

Now all he had to do was decide which member to pick off, and let the games begin. Zaun was riding on the back of one sled; the woman driving had to be Maria. Jack was operating the other machine, but who was behind him?

Decisions, decisions, Cable thought.

He finally decided, took aim, and fired.

Something jolted the snowmobile. Jack thought he might've run over a large piece of debris buried in the snow, but then the sled's engine started smoking and sputtered to a halt.

"What happened?" Jill asked.

"I have no—" Jack began when he heard what sounded like a rifle shot. Jill was thrown from the snowmobile as if by an invisible force. Maria pulled up next to him. She was pointing to his right.

"We got a shooter," she yelled over her sled's idling engine.

They were easy targets, completely out in the open. Instinct took over. "Get out of here," he yelled, frantically waving for Maria to speed off.

"Not without you," she said. "Come on."

Jack saw Jill's form lying in the snow, a huge hole in the side of her helmet. The snow was reddening around it. He knew she was dead. His sled was finished. He stepped over the seat, ready to hop onto the back of Maria's machine, Zaun having scooted up on the seat, when another shot rang out. Jack felt immense pressure in his upper thigh as he was twirled around like a rag doll and tossed onto the snowy ground, the bullet's impact having a sledgehammer-like affect.

Pain engulfed his right leg. Looking down, he saw blood spurting from where he was hit. He looked at Maria and Zaun. They were sitting ducks, ready to be shot down like himself and Jill. "Get out of here now!"

Another gunshot sounded and a piece of exposed seat burst apart, the yellow foam cushion cascading the area.

Zaun reached for Jack, but he was too far away. Jack saw his friend attempt to rise and get off the machine, but Maria held Zaun back with her arm.

"Get to someplace safe," Jack yelled, blood gushing from his leg. He hoped Maria's smarts would kick in, the woman a trained military personnel knowing that to stay where she was would mean certain death for them all. A moment later, Maria hit the gas on the sled. The tread spun, kicking up snow and covering Jack in the fluffy white stuff.

His leg was in bad shape. He was bleeding out. The bullet must have hit his femoral artery.

More gunshots rang out, but Jack heard Maria and Zaun's snowmobile, which meant it was still operational. Good.

He lay there, exposed, waiting to be finished off, but the killing shot never came. He wondered what the shooter was waiting for. He arched his neck and saw Jill's body. Poor girl. But his sympathy quickly turned to terror when he saw the first zombie. It stopped at Jill's corpse, knelt down, and ripped her clothing away to get at the meat. Three more quickly joined in, the zombies obviously alerted by the noise of snowmobiles and gunshots.

Reaching down, Jack pulled his .45 from its holster, the M4 still on the sled. Resting the gun on his chest, he pulled out his knife and sliced off the sleeve of his jacket and wrapped it tightly around his leg to slow the bleeding, then cut a strip of his sleeve and made a tourniquet above the wound. Maybe it'd buy him a little more time, give Maria and Zaun a chance to find the son-of-a-bitch and kill him, then get back to him. He'd like to be around long enough to see that they were safe. And even though he was losing a lot of blood, he couldn't give up trying.

Feeling the icy cold of winter creeping into his bones, he crawled to the sled's engine and leaned against it, feeling a modicum of security by the heavy machine. The plastic engine cover was warm, the heat a blessing, but he knew it wouldn't last long.

Damn, he'd lost so much blood already.

Now, all he could do was make sure he remained awake, and defend himself. He'd wait for his friends to return after they took out the shooter. Deep down, he knew even if they did this, the probability of him lasting long enough to see them again wasn't good. But he had hope, which was about all he had left.

Movement from his left caught his attention. Jack raised his gun arm and blew a hole in the zombie's head. Another came from his right. He adjusted his aim and fired, missing his mark. He fired again, this time downing the thing as its brains flew from its skull.

He could do this. He could fend them off. It was better than waiting without anything to do, he thought, almost laughing. Another zombie was coming. He raised the weapon and fired, but the bullet went wide as he was attacked from behind, the stench of rot falling over him. He felt the corpse's teeth sink into the side of his neck. Jack brought the gun back, pressed the barrel against the thing's head, closed his eyes, and pulled the trigger. The zombie fell away, dead forever this time. A warm sensation spread over his neck and he knew the zombie had broken the skin. If the leg wound didn't kill him, maybe the bite would.

The zombie that had been coming for him turned and joined the others that were eating Jill. He laughed, enjoying the bit of luck that finally swung his way. Exhausted, he lay back, breathing hard. He wasn't ready to leave this world, but sometimes things just didn't go as expected.

Another zombie was walking toward him. Jack smiled. He raised the .45 and fired.

THE END
(or is it?)

NIGHTMARE OF THE DEAD
VINCENZO BILOF

In a world of war and mayhem, a twisted nightmare of undead cannibals begins.

The outlaw Neasa Bannan uncovers a horrifying conspiracy engineered by the psychopathic mastermind behind the Confederacy's deadly flesh-hungry weapons. A homicidal gunslinger and a brotherhood of killers emerge out of Neasa's tragic, blood-soaked past while the living dead ravage the land.

With the fate of the country in the balance, Neasa must decide: save the Union from the undead menace, or surrender to Saul's vision of ultra-violence.

www.severedpress.com

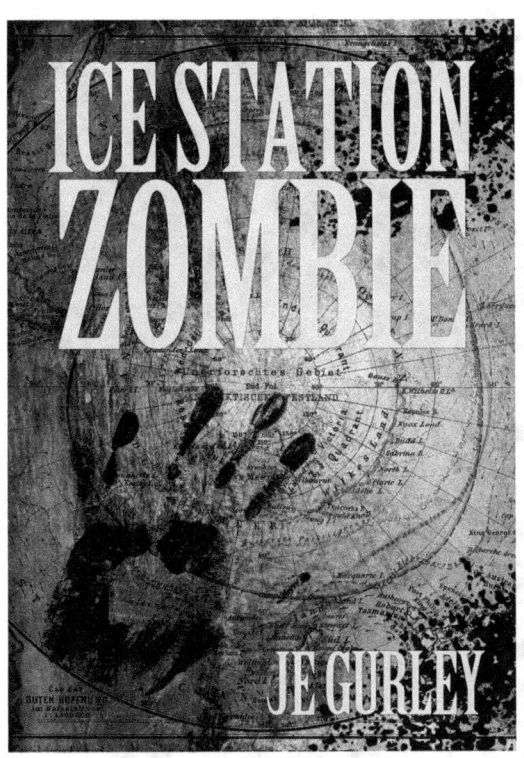

ICE STATION ZOMBIE
JE GURLEY

For most of the long, cold winter, Antarctica is a frozen wasteland. Now, the ice is melting and the zombies are thawing. Arctic explorers Val Marino and Elliot Anson race against time and death to reach Australia, but the Demise has preceded them and zombies stalk the streets of Adelaide and Coober Pedy.

www.severedpress.com

The Coalition

When the dead rose to destroy the living, Ron Cutter learned to survive. While so many others died, he thrived. His life is a constant battle against the living dead. As he casts his own bullets and packs his shotgun shells, his humanity slowly melts away.

Then he encounters a lost boy and a woman searching for a place of refuge. Can they help him recover the emotions he set aside to live? And if he does recover them, will those feelings be an asset in his struggles, or a danger to him?

THE STATE OF EXTINCTION: the first installment in the **COALITON OF THE LIVING** trilogy of Mankind's battle against the plague of the Living Dead. As recounted by author **Robert Mathis Kurtz.**

www.severedpress.com

MACHINES OF THE DEAD

The dead are rising. The island of Manhattan is quarantined. Helicopters guard the airways while gunships patrol the waters. Bridges and tunnels are closed off. Anyone trying to leave is shot on sight.

For Jack Warren, survival is out of his hands when a group of armed military men kidnap him and his infected wife from their apartment and bring them to a bunker five stories below the city.

There, Jack learns a terrible truth and the reason why the dead have risen. With the help of a few others, he must find a way to escape the bunker and make it out of the city alive.

JUDGMENT DAY

Dr. Jebediah Stone never believed in zombies until he had to shoot one. Now they're mutating into a new species, capable of reproducing, and the only defence is 'Blue Juice', a vaccine distilled from the blood of rare individuals immune to the zombie plague. Dr. Stone's missing wife is one of these unwilling 'munies', snatched by the military under the Judgment Day Protocol.It's a new, dangerous world filled with zombies, street gangs, and merciless Hunters desperate for a shot of blue juice. Has the world turned on mankind? Is Mortuus Venator the new ruler of earth?

TIMOTHY
MARK TUFO

Timothy was not a good man in life and being
undead did little to improve his disposition.
Find out what a man trapped in his own mind
will do to survive when he wakes up to find
himself a zombie controlled by a self-aware
virus

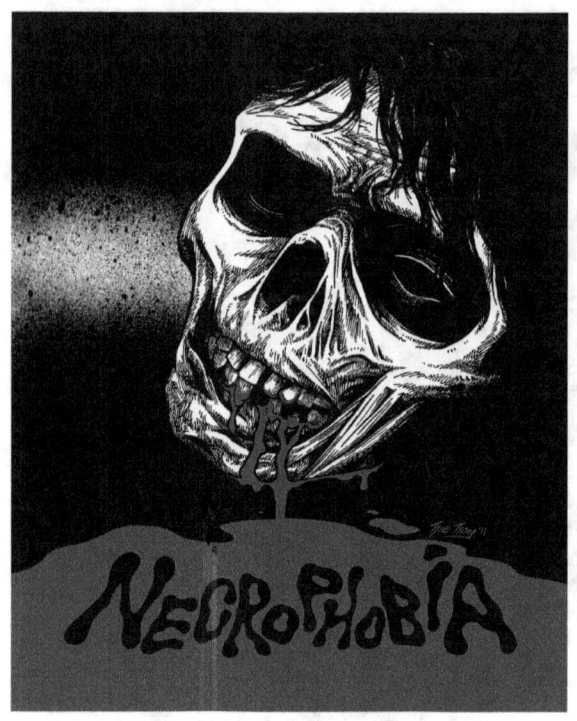

NECROPHOBIA

An ordinary summer's day.
The grass is green, the flowers are blooming. All is right with the
world. Then the dead start rising. From cemetery and mortuary,
funeral home and morgue, they flood into the streets until every
town and city is infested with walking corpses, blank-eyed
eating machines that exist to take down the living.
The world is a graveyard.
And when you have a family to protect, it's more than survival.
It's war.

Zombie Fallout
Mark Tufo
CURRENTLY IN DEVELOPMENT WITH
Illuminandi Media
ShaedStudios.com